MY [illegible], MY ADDICTION

JAMIE KYLE MCGILLIAN

Printed in the United States of America

ISBN: Softcover 978-1-63871-662-4
eBook 978-1-63871-680-8

Republished by: PageTurner Press and Media LLC
Publication Date: 10/28/2021

To order copies of this book, contact:
PageTurner Press and Media
Phone: 1-888-447-9651
info@pageturner.us
www.pageturner.us

TO MY LOVES

Bailey and Devan

Chapter One

Jack is Back

As I walk to my car, I wonder if he is watching me from the window of Starbucks. I try to walk my best. I try not to trip. I try to walk like a strong woman. Like someone who has their life together. Yep, that's it. I got some rhythm in my step now. When I reach my car, I slide in and pull out as fast as I can. Breathe! In and out. I don't go directly to the mall to meet Becky. I pull over on a street near Starbucks to collect my thoughts. I just sit there with my hot mochaccino that Jack just bought for me and I try to remember how to breathe. This is no easy task. He was so sublime! He was *so* Jack. My Jack. It has been five months since I have seen him. I didn't know he would be back. I thought he was gone forever. Who knew that I would just run into him at the very place where we first met?

I can't help but think about the last time we were together. His parents were making him leave New York, leave me, and head to California. He was in trouble. He needed an intervention.

Uncle Aiden was going to help him stop drinking. It was a last-ditch effort. They had tried everything else. Jack just couldn't control the problem. We were both crying. I had never seen a guy cry before. Well, I was hysterical. Jack was shedding a few tears. But Jack was scared out of his mind. He didn't want to go, didn't want to leave me, but he knew he had a problem and it wasn't going away on its own. It was just growing like a cancer.

I guess I saw signs of it from the very beginning, but sometimes, you just don't want to see something. It reminds me of this beautiful blue dress I bought a few years ago. I wanted it so badly that I refused to see that the material was pulled along the seam. It was the last one on the rack, and even though I saw the imperfection, I didn't acknowledge it. I pretended it wasn't there. I brought it home and tried it on and my mom said, "It's lovely, Lace, but it's frayed on the seam." I saw it, and yet, I didn't. But Jack was so perfect in every other way. And let's face it, doesn't every eighteen–year-old boy drink whenever he gets the opportunity? For the last two years from ninth grade to eleventh, hasn't it been every guy's mission to get wasted? That's what makes you popular. I mean, I don't believe that, of course, but that's just the way it is. I didn't make the rules. Jack didn't make the rules. He was just following them.

I don't blame Jack's parents for wanting to help him. They love him and they want what's best for him. He is so perfect in every other way. He really should not ruin a brilliant future, just so he can party now. His mother's had a serious drinking problem and she was able to nip it in the bud by getting closer to God. Jack tried that, but it just led him closer to partying. But the way he left me, it was so sudden. One minute we were on the beach blanket, declaring our love for one another and talking about all the things we were going to do together, and the next minute, we were saying goodbye. It was so awful. I never want to have that kind of pain again. After he was gone, my world was empty. I don't ever want to go there again. And Jack doesn't even know what happened after he left. He has no idea what I went through.

We were supposed to have the whole summer. It was going to be my best summer, and instead, it turned into my worst. I am almost a half a year away from it all. I'm different now. Life is different. I am older. And I think about Jack's reaction when he saw me holding my car keys.

He was so happy for me. I'm driving now, which means I'm much more independent. I can do things that I couldn't do when I was with Jack.

It's a lot to take in. His face. His beautiful face that was wiped off the face of social media. His eyes. The mouth. It's all too much for me. I sip my coffee and I am reminded of our times in Starbucks when Jack and I would practically sit on top of each other and just flirt back and forth. Jack's kiss. It took so long to wipe that kiss out of my mind. I would go to sleep pretending that his lips were on mine. I would wake up feeling the emptiness and the longing.

What am I going to do with all of this? If Jack really comes back for good in a month like he said, am I really going to be able to take him back and fit him in my life? Can I do that? Will it work? What happens when he finds out that I have become friends with his friend Mason Cleets? Will he be angry? And what happens when he finds out what happened when he was gone?

I don't feel so good. My belly hurts. It's too much. I need a good song to take me out of this reality. I tune into Elton John. I know, I know, I sound like an old lady. I have old taste when it comes to music. I like what I like and that is all there is to it. As I drive to the mall to meet Becky, I am hoping she will know what to do with all of this.

I am supposed to meet Beck in front of Victoria's Secret, of all places. As I am walking down the mall, I spot her. She is dressed in black jeans, black boots, and a black sweater. Lately, Becky has given up all color. She only wears black, but she's not goth, she's just Becky. She's got her arms around Hoff. No surprise there. They are inseparable now. The hot couple of the moment. They are the tall couple. Hoff is sticking his tongue down Beck's throat and she is loving it. What an appropriate scene outside Victoria's Secret! If that doesn't make you feel like buying a thong, I don't know what does. Becky sees me coming toward her out of the corner of her eye, and she knows something is not right. She just knows. It's a best-friend thing. She pulls away from Hoff, who is obviously disappointed, left standing there with his tongue sticking out of his mouth.

"What did you do?" she asks.

I shake my head. I don't want to ruin their moment, and I also don't want to get in the way of black Friday shopping. The mall is already filled with eager shoppers on the hunt for bargains.

"You look like you've just seen a ghost," Becky says, and then she burps. Good old Becky.

"Oh no. Is it your mom? Is she having the baby?"

"No. Not yet." I shake my head.

Mom is due in less than a week.

Becky walks toward me and touches my hands. "You're shaking."

"It's all right. I'm cold. I'm good."

Becky turns to Hoff. "Hoff, you've got to get out of here. Start shopping, boy. Lacey needs me. Meet you here in exactly two hours. Got it?" she says.

Hoff winks and nods his head. "Got it, Beck! Hope everything is all right, Lace," he says.

"Thanks, Hoff. Did you have a nice Thanksgiving?" I say. I try to make small talk, because, really, Hoff used to be such an ass, but for some reason, now he's a genuinely good guy.

Hoff nods.

"It's about that guy, Jack, isn't it?" he asks me. "How did you know?" I ask.

"I can tell. It's all over your face. You've just seen him, haven't you?" I nod and Becky gasps and it's creepy.

"Happy shopping, ladies!" Hoff winks at Becky, and then he is gone. "No way!" Becky says. "No way, no way, no way!"

She's really loud and making a big scene, and I just hate when she does that. "No way. No way." She keeps saying it.

"Let's get some coffee and talk about this, Lace. We've got to be strong. I'm here to help you, girl!" I nod. I could use some help.

"I think Hoff has ESP. He knows things, you know?" Becky asks.

I nod. I don't know if Hoff has ESP, or if my heartache is written all over my face.

Becky puts her arm around me and walks me to the coffee kiosk. She plants me in a seat and gets in line to get me my fave, vanilla latte. "And let's make it a decaf," says Becky.

I sit and try to gather my thoughts. I have to say, even though Becky is not going to be happy about this, and she's going to tell me that it is best not to pick up the pieces with Jack, I am so into the thought of kissing Jack again. I am only human. I am having just the tiniest Jack attack. Right here and right now.

The Jack attack: You're in the middle of living your life. Maybe you are at the mall, or watching a TV show, or playing Hangman. Maybe you are making a cup of tea for your mom, who is very pregnant. Maybe you are getting ready for bed. All of a sudden, you feel a flutter, then a chill up your spine. You hear the word, Jack. All your senses numb. You can't believe that this world, which contains beautiful things, such as diamonds, coffee, the moon and the stars, ocean breezes, Good and Plenty, and sweet little babies, also contains Jack. Jack. That crazy, mad boy who loved me once. The boy with the mad dimples, who makes me smile until my face hurts.

Jack attack. You don't want to be operating heavy machinery during a Jack attack. You don't want to be behind the wheel or hammering a nail.

When the Jack attack passes, you just want to be very still and let it drift over you until you return to the planet.

"Spill," Becky is shouting.

"All right," I say, annoyed by Becky's persistence.

She has bought herself a cinnamon danish and she is shoving it in her mouth and chewing with her mouth open. This is usual for Becky. Her table manners suck. I look away.

"I went to Starbucks before meeting you. I was standing in line. He tapped me from behind. There he was. As soon as I saw him, my heart started to race. He was right there in front of me, after all this time. It's so crazy. He looked different," I say, sipping my coffee and looking at the crowds of shoppers.

"Different how?" Becky asks.

"Leaner, and his hair is really short. Almost like a crew cut. He looks like he's been running a lot. He's not as big as he used to be," I say. "You know, not as bulky."

"What did he say, Lace? Why didn't he call or connect? What the hell did the bum say?"

"It wasn't like that. Not being in touch with me, with anyone, was part of the treatment," I say.

"That sounds like bullshit. Just because you need to go away because you are drinking like a fish, doesn't mean you can't drop a line to your girlfriend," Becky says.

Immediately, I wish I were alone. Becky doesn't get it.

"Love means never having to say you're sorry," I stupidly mutter. Becky rolls her eyes and stares at me.

"You know what?" I say.

"What?" says Beck.

But I don't say anything. I don't want to get into a fight with her over this. "Is he back for good?" she asks.

"Not yet. He's coming home for Christmas. For good. As long as he sticks to his program," I say.

"Well, isn't that just great?" Becky says, sarcastically.

I don't say anything. I want to end the conversation, not get Becky all excited.

"What happens after Christmas? Are you going to take it where you left off?" Becky asks. I shrug my shoulders. I really don't know.

"What? Now you're not going to talk about this, Lace?" she asks. I shrug my shoulders again.

"I am only trying to protect you," she says.

I nod. I know that. Beck has my back. I know she is just thinking about what is best for me. That's what I'm thinking about. All I come up with is Jack.

"May I remind you about the girl who came home from the hospital who could hardly speak? How it took weeks to get you out just to go for ice cream? Do you remember that girl?"

I nod. I do remember that girl. I don't want to go there again.

"Listen to me," says Becky. She's pointing her finger in my face now. "I'm going to do everything I can to make sure that you don't get hurt."

I nod. I remind myself that Becky means well. But I want her finger out of my face.

"Please, Becky, don't be so hard on me," I say, and I can feel a tear running down my face. "Shit! Now you're going to weep?" she asks.

"Please, Becky! It was so good to see him. He is so beautiful. He has this calm about him now. I think he really is going to be all right. You know, with the drinking thing."

Becky doesn't say anything.

I shut my eyes. I know it's not a good situation. If Jack comes back, how can things be all right? What happens if he drinks again? Then they'll send him away, and I will have to survive that all over again. But this is Jack we are talking about. Jack!

Becky is looking in her purse for something. She takes out a tissue and hands it to me, but as I go to take it, I see that the tissue has lipstick all over it.

"Sorry. Gross!" Becky exclaims, and throws the tissue back in her bag. She passes me a napkin with a few crumbs on it.

I smile. Beck is my best friend and I know she wants me to be happy.

"Give me a hug. Stand up. Let everyone here think we are lesbians. I don't give a shit," she says. I laugh. I stand and hug her.

"Let's talk about it later, all right?" she asks. "Now it's time to shop 'til we drop."

That's exactly what I want her to say. For now, I have a whole bunch of things I need to buy for Christmas.

The first thing I need to get is something for the baby, who of course, is not here yet, but is expected to make her appearance any day now. Mom is so tired and swollen, she can't even get off the couch, so I told her I would take care of everything. It's the least I can do. If I can have some Christmas gifts ready to go, it will be one less thing Mom has to worry about.

At the Gap, I find the most adorable pink velvet dress. It blows my mind. All the baby clothes look like doll clothes. I settle on the pink dress, a powder blue sleeper, and two pairs of wool tights. At the register, I throw in a few hair ribbons and some booties. The stuff is expensive, but adorable.

My next stop is The Sports Authority. This is for, Breckinridge, who I now call James. I need to buy my own gift for James, and also a gift from my mom. I buy him a pair of sneakers and a whistle. I think that's perfect, because he is the gym teacher, and don't all gym teachers wear sneakers and carry whistles? From my mom, I buy James a sweat suit, a basketball, six pairs of socks, and two pairs of gym shorts. It's not ideal, but it's something.

At Victoria's Secret, I buy Mom Pink sweat pants and a sweatshirt. I also buy her a comfy nightgown. I know she will love it. I buy Becky some perfume and a candle, while she is busy trying something on for her sister. Then we go to a candy store and a pet store. I buy Gramps some chocolate and a few doggy treats for Rosey-O. Then I go to Starbucks and get a pound of coffee and a green mug. This is a just in case gift. Just in case I need a gift for Jack. Just in case. Becky doesn't say anything to me. She doesn't have to. She knows that I know that she knows that I am a lovesick idiot. Lovesick idiots always need to buy just-in-case gifts.

Hoff is standing in front of Victoria's Secret where we left him. He is carrying a bunch of shopping bags, including one from Victoria's Secret, and as we walk toward him, Becky is trying to speculate what could be in the bag. Hoff and Becky want me to go to lunch with them and even though I really don't want to, I agree, because I don't want any hard feelings between me and Becky.

We go to the Food Court, because that is the only place I can afford, and I get a salad. Becky gets a huge plate of Chinese food, and Hoff gets a burger and fries from Wendy's. Becky says that my lunch is the only healthy one, but I disagree with her, because my salad is dripping with dressing. The mood is light and even though the food court is packed with shoppers, I am glad I went to lunch with them.

"It's official. Christmas season has begun," Hoff says. "I can't believe it," I say, and I really can't.

"This is the first year that I don't really want anything. I feel like I have everything. You know?" Becky says.

Is she joking? Usually, Becky is wanting everything at the Mac store, at Forever Twenty-one, at Pottery Barn, and at Anthropologie. Maybe this year she really is different. Maybe she is no longer a material girl.

"Babe, I'm glad you feel that way, because I don't have much money," Hoff says.

They both laugh. Becky puts her arm around Hoff. They really do make a sweet couple.

Hoff eats with his mouth closed and his napkin on his lap. He's a really nice guy and I think Becky is lucky that she waited for Hoff to come around. Becky eats with her mouth wide open and from time to time, she burps. Disgusting!

"My dad and I were talking last night and he told me that his salary was chopped in half this year. He said that we have to make some changes and it starts with the holidays. We have to simplify," Becky says. "I can do that!" Becky puts down her fork and smiles.

"It's not the end of the world. Christmas is really about friends and family. Think about my Christmas this year," and as I say it, I feel a tingle up my spine.

I am referring to Mom's baby, but I can't help thinking about Jack, as well. I will see him for Christmas.

"I know. You're so lucky. It's going to be fun being a big sister," Becky smiles.

"Fun, but loud. I hope for your sake, that baby is a good sleeper, you know?" Hoff asks. He's a really nice guy, but he is no rocket scientist.

"You're right, Hoff," I say.

Hoff is in a good mood and Becky seems really happy. We are not talking about Jack. That's a good thing, because I am starting to feel exhausted. I am finding it hard to believe that I actually saw him this morning. Maybe it wasn't real. Maybe it was just a dream. Maybe I am losing my mind.

But I do have proof. I have the empty coffee cup from the hot chocolate that Jack bought me. It's in my car. And then I remember Jack's face and his hands and his eyes, and I know that it was definitely real. Just then, I get a text from my mom, who is just checking in, and is asking me to bring her something to eat. She says she's starving even though she ate like an hour ago. She wants tacos. I laugh out loud.

"Mom is totally craving," I say.

"What does Kate want today?" Becky asks, as she shoves her fork in her mouth. Becky is so thin and so tall, she can just eat and eat, and never gain an ounce.

"She wants tacos."

Beck has to lend me a few dollars so I can get Mom two tacos and an order of chips and salsa. As I walk through the mall with all my shopping bags, I see all the wreaths, the twinkling lights, and the wrapped gifts in the store windows. There's so much expectation during the holiday season. There's also disappointment. And, is it really necessary to play Christmas music when it's still November? Come on, people! Lighten up! I just finished looking at pumpkins, for God's sake. Let me ease into it. Urgh!

CHAPTER TWO

Mom's About to Burst

When I get home, Mom is on the couch and James is rubbing her feet. She looks tremendous. Her face is swollen and her feet are out of proportion. It's scary to see her like this.

James stands up and helps me with the packages.

"Is that your Mom's taco?" he asks, pointing to the bag with a picture of a red hot chili pepper. I nod and he grabs the bag and goes into the kitchen to set it on a plate.

I look over at Mom. She is so ready to get that baby out. I don't know what I can do to help her, but I do know that I don't need to do anything to add to her stress level. She doesn't need to know that I saw Jack this morning. She doesn't need to know that it felt like my heart was going to come out of my chest. She doesn't need to know that I have already thought about what it would feel like to kiss him again. There's no reason to tell her any of this.

"Are you okay, Lace?" she asks.

I find it hard to believe that she is so ready to give birth now, but she is thinking about whether or not I am okay.

I nod and take a seat next to her on the couch. "Are *you* okay?" I ask.

She nods and then she laughs. "Yes and no! How was shopping?"

"It's officially Christmas season. The crowds have begun. Not too many bargains, but lots of lines," I say. "I managed to spend every penny I had."

She smiles. "Well, I owe you money for some stuff. I'll give it to you as soon as I can get up. Did you get something for James from me?" she whispers.

"Of course," I nod. "You're good to go and I even have wrapping paper and I will take care of it all."

She puts her hands on her belly.

"Any time now," she says. "Let's do this thing," she says. "Are you scared, Mom?" I ask.

Mom takes a minute to think about my question.

"I can't lie to you. I *am* scared. I was scared with you. That was so long ago."

James comes from the kitchen carrying a plate of tacos. He is smiling ear to ear, but I can tell that he is nervous. Unlike my mother, he has never done this before. This baby will be his first.

"Enjoy, babe," he says. He sits across from us and studies my mom. "James, you're not going to stare at me, are you?"

James looks hurt, but then he smiles.

We all laugh. James is so tense these last few days. He doesn't know what to do with himself, but he is so sweet and kind about it. My mom couldn't be happier to be having James' baby. I just know that, and it makes me happy. She had years of loneliness, and now, she is finally with someone special. Mom and James have given me a hopeful feeling. Like there really is someone out there for everyone. Oops, I get a surge of Jack. I can feel him.

"Show me what you got for the baby?" Mom asks.

"Are you sure? You don't want it to be a surprise?" I ask. "Show me, Lacey. Please."

I don't know if I should show Mom the baby clothes. I look to James to give me his take on it.

"Why not?" he asks. "At this point, we want to do whatever makes your mom happy."

So I take out the pink velvet dress and the booties and the hair ribbons and the blue sleeper. Mom is making a lot of cooing noises. James is holding up the dress against his body.

"For three to six months," James says, as he reads the label. "So tiny! Who can be this teeny?" James exclaims.

And just like that we are all so happy and excited about what is to come with our old/new family. Mom eats her entire taco plate. No surprise there. James eats the chips and salsa. I go to my room to process everything that has happened today. I decide my best way of dealing with seeing Jack this morning is to write about it in my journal.

I write about how surreal it was. I write how I wasn't expecting to see him again. I write about how I wonder if it's possible to turn this all around and make a happy ending. I write about what I know about this guy, this boy, who came into my life and made me feel so happy and so sad.

Jack is back and I am flying on a magic carpet ride across the sky. Jack is my drug and I want to shoot him up inside me. I take out the silver heart necklace he gave me. I won't put it on. That will complicate things too much, but I just hold it in my hand and rub the silver chain back and forth between my fingers.

After a dinner of, what else, turkey leftovers, Mom is still on the couch and James and I are doing the dishes.

"I don't want turkey ever again," I say. James nods.

"Turkey gets a bad rap for the rest of the year because everyone eats so much of it at Thanksgiving," says James.

"So, do we have a plan?" I ask James, changing the subject abruptly.

"What do you mean?" James asks. He is looking at me with a blank face as he holds up a soapy dish in his hands.

"When the time comes," I explain.

James finally gets what I am talking about. He starts nodding frantically.

"In as much as we can have a plan. Monday she goes to the doctor. Actually, would you mind driving her? It's early in the morning. If you can do it, I can take Gramps to his doctor's appointment."

"Sure, no prob," I say.

I want to help. Now that I have a license, I can definitely take Mom to a doctor's appointment. I'm happy to do that and it makes me feel like a grown up. An adult. It is a welcome change.

We agree to take it from there. The doctor should be able to let us know when the baby will be coming.

I get a text from Mason that he's on his way over. Usually, I let Mason read my writing because he is a fellow writer, but I will not show him what I wrote about Jack. Mason is a good friend of Jack's. That's how we met. I like Mason as a friend. But I think Mason wants more.

I am in the kitchen making my mom a cup of tea when Mason comes. He is carrying his skateboard and a bag of brownies that his mom has made for us.

As I make the tea, Mason is going on about how his mom burned the turkey and how they had fourteen dinner guests. His dad ended up having to cook quesadillas for everyone. Mason is really shy in front of my mom and James. He just won't talk when they come in the room. He nods and smiles. It's a little strange. The kid is in twelfth grade and he's still afraid of adults. Not so good.

We take a walk because it's a beautiful night. Mason and I are eating the brownies. I don't tell Mason that they taste burnt. Poor Mrs. Cleets. She never gets it right.

"You saw him, right?"

"Who?" I ask.

"Jack. Don't be coy, Lace. I know you saw him."

"Then why are you asking me?"

Mason is sitting in the park smoking a joint. I am sitting across from him. It never occurred to me that Mason would know that Jack was in town for Thanksgiving.

"So what if I did, Mase?" I ask.

"Don't do it, Lace. Don't fall for him. He's a drunk. You're too good for him," Mason says, as he hits hard on the joint.

"You've got to be kidding me," I say. Mason looks at me.

"I thought Jack was your friend. Is that anyway to talk about a friend? Call him a drunk?" I ask. "Come on. You know what I'm saying," says Mason.

"No I don't. What if he said you were a total stoner?" I ask. "That's different and you know it," Mason says.

Mason's long dark hair covers his left eye.

"You know how much I care about you. We are good friends. I was thinking we could maybe take it to the next step. But we can't do that if you let Jack back in."

I stare at Mason. He's cute, but he looks like a child, carrying his skateboard around, hitting on the joint.

"Think about it, Lacey. We could be really good together."

He's here to tell me that I shouldn't fall for Jack again. As if Jack is getting in his way. As if. I get up from my bench because I feel angry, and I don't want to sit and watch Mason get high.

"You don't know what you're talking about. How did you know I saw him?" I said.

"Word gets around. Nobo told me."

Nobo is another friend of Jack's. Not the sharpest tool in the shed. I nod. I cross my arms against my chest. My mom tells me I do this when I am angry and I don't want to listen to what the other person has to say. She's definitely right about that.

"Mason, you know how I feel about you. Nothing is going to change that."

Mason blows out a billow of smoke. He stands and walks toward me. He puts his hands on my hips.

"What are you doing?" I ask.

"Just give me a chance. I can make you so happy, Lace. With me, you know what you're getting. No surprises. Come on. We can be so good together. Two writers together."

Now Mason is trying to press his lips against mine. "No!" I shout. "What the hell?" I push Mason away. "What the fuck, Lacey?" says Mason. He shrinks back.

I wipe my mouth with the back of my hand.

"Gross!" I shudder.

We don't talk for a while. I am not sure what to do with this. If I tell him off it may be the end of our friendship. If I wait a bit, and then explain that I don't feel that way toward him, maybe we can still salvage something. Truth is, I like Mason. Just, not in that way. I never had a friend who I could share my writing with. I never had a friend who I could brainstorm story ideas with. It's been a great diversion.

"Look," Mason says, but then he doesn't say anything else. I just kind of wait there until he finishes his sentence. Awkward.

"I'm sorry. It's not worth risking our friendship. If you aren't into me that way, I can't make it happen," he says.

"That's right, Mason. You can't."

"Do you forgive me?" he asks.

I don't know if I can.

"I think so. Just calm down, Mason. The Jack thing is very hard for me. I don't know what to say about it. I'm kind of thinking that I am going to take from now until Christmas to see what I want to do about Jack. And it's nobody's business."

"I don't want you to get hurt," he says. "Jack *will* hurt you. I can tell you that. He acts like he is in control and everyone loves Jack. But then he goes and fucks up. It always happens," Mason says.

I glare at Mason.

"You know I'm right," he whispers. "No I don't."

"Jack is always looking like he's perfect, but he's not," says Jack.

"Thanks, Mason. I'm a big girl. I can make my own decisions. I can handle it."

I go to take Mason's hand, but then I forget that idea. I don't want to send mixed signals now.

There was a time when I considered it totally normal to hold his hand, or put my arm around him, but now I know that he won't be able to deal with that.

"Let me tell you about my latest sci-fi story," he begins. "It is the future. Humans are obsolete. The only life forms are the Beons and the Seenits. The Beons look like regular people as we know them, but they have tremendous powers. They can change their size. One minute they can be the size of a coffee cup, and the next minute they can be the size of the Empire State Building. The Seenits are the descendants of humans. They are very small creatures who do not have any powers. Seenits are simpletons. They are like the people who lived in the Dark Ages. They don't read or think. But, if a Beon has sex with a Seenit, a third life form is created called a Glowgon. A Glowgon can do some really amazing things. Glowgons have all kinds of powers, but every once in a while a Glowgon goes bad."

"I like it. So there's sex in your story?" I ask. "Typical."

Mason smiles. "Of course there's sex in it. Sex, drugs, and rock n'roll!" he shouts.

"You're insane," I say and we both laugh. A throaty chuckle comes out of Mason's mouth.

We walk out of the park and back to my house. We don't bring up Jack's name again for the rest of the night.

On Monday morning, I am taking Mom to her doctor's appointment. She is moving very slowly. I hold her hand as we walk to the car because there is frost on the ground. If she falls, she may never get up. I try to keep the mood light. I don't have to be at school until 10:35, and her appointment is at nine, so there shouldn't be any problems.

When we get to the doctor's office, I worry because Mom is definitely the puffiest woman in the place. There are some other very pregnant women in the waiting room, but they don't look anywhere near as large as Mom.

When the nurse sees Mom, she immediately asks her to come into room one. I escort Mom into the room and help her sit on the table. The first thing the nurse does is take Mom's blood pressure. This is pretty standard and Mom is looking relatively relaxed.

I can tell that the nurse is a bit alarmed by the reading of Mom's blood pressure. She takes it again and writes something down in Mom's file.

"Now, Mrs. Breckinridge, I need you to pee in the cup."

The nurse is an older woman who doesn't seem to have any time for small talk. I help my mother waddle into the bathroom so that she can pee in a cup. As I stand outside the bathroom door, I am getting a creepy feeling. Something is not right.

Before my mom comes out of the bathroom, the nurse walks by and asks me to step inside room one. Now I am scared. I do not know what to think. She leads me into the room and shuts the door.

"What's your name, dear?" she asks. She actually smiles this time, and I feel a little better. "Lacey. Is my mom all right?" I ask, trying to keep the tone casual.

"Well, she has severe edema and high blood pressure," she says.

"That translates to what?" I ask politely.

"It's called preeclampsia. It happens when there's swelling, or edema, high blood pressure, and protein in the urine."

"What's it mean?" I ask, my heart pounding out of my chest.

"It means that baby has to be born soon. Your mom has to be checked into the hospital right away. We will need to monitor her vitals and the baby's vitals, and we will probably have to induce labor."

"Shit! I mean, sorry! I curse when I get nervous, sometimes," I say. I am such a jerk.

"It's all right. I don't want to alarm your mom. That will only make things worse. That's why I am telling you this now. When she comes out of the bathroom, I am going to explain that it's time for her to check into the hospital. The doctor will meet you there and we'll go from there. Now, where is your dad?"

I give the nurse a cold, blank stare. I have no idea where that asshole is. Last I heard he was in Vegas, but he could be in Scotland for all I know.

"Why do you need to know that? We don't really communicate," I explain. The nurse looks at me with a puzzled face.

"That's odd. I know I've met him," she says. She picks up Mom's chart and skims it. What the hell is this bitch talking about?

"Where is Mr. Breckinridge?" she asks.

"Oh!" I nod. "Now I got you. The baby's father! Sorry about that. Umm, he should be around. He was taking my Gramps to a doctor's appointment."

"Can you reach him and have him meet you at the hospital?"

Yes. I take out my phone from the front pocket of my jeans and I start texting James: **Mom needs to go to hospital now. Blood pressure high. Let's not mention it to her. Meet you at hospital.**

Within five minutes, James texts me back:

OMG! Be there as soon as I can!

Poor James. He is probably a nervous wreck.

The door of room one opens and another nurse who is quite large is helping my mom waddle into the room. It's quite a sight.

"That was a production! I'm exhausted," Mom says quietly.

The first nurse, who I see now is wearing a name tag with the name *Nancy* written on it, is telling mom that it's time to go to the hospital and have the baby.

"Hon, your pressure is high and there is protein in your urine," Nancy says. "Preeclampsia?" Mom asks.

Nancy nods and tries to make light of it when she sees that Mom is alarmed.

"Kate, we are going to get you settled in a labor room, put you on a magnesium drip and see where we are going to go from there. Do you understand?" Nancy asks.

I squeeze my mom's hand. I try to act like this is normal procedure.

"We're good to go, Mom. We'll get you checked in and then I'll go home and bring your overnight bag, and James will meet us at the hospital."

Mom looks at me. She knows that while she's been peeing, plans have been made. She looks nervous.

"Mom, it's going to be all right. I promise," I say. Please God, let it be all right.

Mom nods.

It takes forever for me to get Mom out of the doctor's office and back into the car. By the time she is in the car, she is breathing hard, and she looks exhausted. I am breathing hard and I look exhausted. It's then that I realize that my poor mother is wearing flip flops on the second to last day in November.

"Mom, why are you wearing flip flops?" I ask.

"I couldn't get my fat foot in a shoe," she shouts. "That's why I am wearing fucking flip flops!"and then she begins to cry.

Mom is freaking out, and I am in charge of getting her to the hospital. My fingers are practically trembling. I don't want her to see. She has to think that I am in control, and that she is going to be fine.

"Let's go meet Daisy," I say, putting on my seatbelt.

Mom knows she is having a girl and they have already decided on the name Daisy. "It's all going to be fine, Mom. Please, just believe me," I say.

"Oh really?" she asks. "That's right," I say.

"How do you know it's going to be fine?"

"Because I just know it, Mom. You have to believe me." Mom's phone rings. She rummages through her purse to find it.

"I hate this purse," she says. She is fishing around in her big leather satchel. She finally finds the phone.

"James?" Mom sounds like she is going to cry.

Mom looks relieved to be talking to her husband. I am relieved that she is relieved.

She says the word *preeclampsia* and James must have read about it in the pregnancy books because he is familiar with the term. He explains that he has Gramps with him, and they are on enroute to the hospital. In fact, they will probably get there before us, because I am having trouble putting the key in the ignition and actually moving the car. It's just a little brain fart. I tell myself that I can do this. I've had my license for a few months already, and there is nothing challenging to the drive to the hospital. It's about five miles, and, really, any moron can do it. I just need to get the car out of park and into drive.

James puts Gramps on the phone and I am not so sure that is a good idea. Gramps always makes Mom so jittery. But it seems like it might be having a calming effect on Mom. She's listening to Gramps, and nodding. At times, she is even laughing, and saying things like, "I remember that, Dad."

We are finally at the hospital and I am trying to get Mom out of the car, but I think we need a forklift. I see James rushing toward us and I have never been so happy to see him. He takes over and I can tell that Mom relaxes in his presence. Gramps is walking slowly toward us. He sees me and he is waving and saying something.

"Gramps!" I say, rushing toward him.

"My love, my honey!" Gramps takes my hand and kisses it. "It's baby time!" he says.

"That's right," I say.

A nurse comes outside to meet us with a wheel chair. It looks like the hospital is expecting us. That makes me even more worried, but I try not to show it. When the chair reaches my mother, she welcomes the chance to sit.

The nurse wheels the chair and takes us through admitting, and to the maternity ward. Gramps looks ready for a nap. I have a hard time catching my breath. I feel like I might vomit. Gramps and I are told to take a seat in the waiting area while James helps Mom get settled in her room. I buy Gramps a cup of tea from the vending machine, but he complains that it tastes like piss. I want to pour it over his head, but instead, I tell him to just close his eyes and take a rest. In no time at all, he is sleeping. I take out my phone and text Becky:

Daisy on the way. Mom has preeclampsia… WTF?

I don't hear back from Beck, which kind of sucks because I really need to talk to someone right now. In a few minutes, James comes out of the room. He looks very pale. I stand up and walk

toward him so that we don't wake Gramps. "How is she? What's happening?" I say.

James has his head in his hands and he is pacing back and forth. "Talk to me!" I say.

"They are putting her on a magnesium sulfate drip. They said she needs to rest. They have to get her pressure down. They attached the fetal monitor. They say the baby is fine. Perfect."

"That's great. We can deal with that," I say. It's a good sign that the baby is doing fine. Little Daisy is fine.

I smile a fake smile.

"This is not like how I imagined it would be. I thought she would just push a little, and then out would come Daisy and then we'd all go home and everything would be perfect," James whispers.

"Have you called your parents?" I ask.

James is nodding. He looks like a timid schoolboy. "I told them to wait before they get a flight" he says. "Just in case it takes longer than we think."

"Oh," I say.

"Thanks, Lace. You're doing great," he says. "Really great." He reaches for my hand and holds it.

"OK, we've got Gramps. Can you take care of him?" I nod.

"Of course I can take care of Gramps."

"She'll need her overnight bag, but that's not so important right now. We can have you get it later. For now, we just have to help her relax and stay calm," he says.

I nod.

"Are you hungry?" I ask.

James looks at me.

"I don't know."

"Well, when was the last time you ate?" I ask.

James explains that he's only had some coffee earlier in the morning. I tell him that I am going to run to the cafeteria to get him a sandwich. He is going to need all his energy. He nods. He says he will sit and watch Gramps while I get the sandwich. He sits down and I walk toward the elevator. Then I realize that I don't have any money with me. I have to go back and ask James for some money. I'm a little embarrassed, but James shakes it off and hands me two twenties. He says I should keep the change because I might need it for later. I get on the elevator and push the up button, but the cafeteria is on the lower level. I have to go all the way up and then down before I get to the cafeteria. When I get to the cafeteria, there is a long line. I go up to the front and ask if I can get a sandwich for my dad, who is not really my dad, but my mom's husband, who is having a baby, and blah, blah, blah. It turns out that everyone in the line has some kind of emergency. That's why we are at the hospital, instead of a restaurant like Panera or the diner. I have to get back to the end of the line and wait my turn. The line isn't too long, but when I get to the front, I almost forget what I am ordering. I get two turkey sandwiches, one for James and one for me and Gramps to split. I figure, I don't want to have to wait in this line again. I get two containers of orange juice and then I am set to get back in the elevator. Suddenly, I can't remember which floor I started on. Was it M for main? Was it L for lobby? I get out at L for lobby and I am very wrong. I walk the whole floor. No maternity ward. I need to get back to the M for main floor, but now I don't know if that is up or down. I find a nurse who looks nice, and I tell her my dilemma. She helps me find the maternity ward. When I get to the waiting area, Gramps is still fast asleep, but James is gone.

I walk around the floor in search of him. I pass my mom's room and look in the doorway. James is sitting at her bedside. Mom is sleeping. I go in, and James smiles at me. I give him his sandwich and his juice. I kiss my mom's hand. Then I go back to the waiting room.

Becky texts me.

Shit babe. Preeclampsia not good. My mom had it. C u soon.

A doctor comes to check in on Mom. Then he talks to me and James outside Mom's door. He explains that Mom is on a magnesium sulfate drip to reduce her risk of having a seizure. He says that soon they will be inducing labor. The baby needs to come out. Mom's blood pressure is very high, but they think they have stabilized it. The baby is still doing fine. He doesn't expect any action for a few hours. It's very important to keep Mom calm now.

My whole body feels twisted. We sit in the waiting room, just as Gramps starts to wake up. He is grouchy when he first wakes up, so we try to give him some time to adjust. James explains the news about Mom.

"I want to see her now," says Gramps, and then he stands and straightens his shirt with his hands. Oh shit.

"I don't know, Gramps," says James. "It may not be the best thing for her and the baby. She has to stay very relaxed."

"But I'm her father," he says. "I know what's best for her."

Gramps is determined to see his daughter. He is not backing down. James doesn't know what to do.

"Gramps, do you promise not to upset Mom?" I ask. "We don't want to do anything to get her tense," I say.

"I won't upset her, Lacey. I want to see my little girl." James looks at me. I shrug my shoulders.

"Five minutes. You have five minutes, Gramps. That's all. I will walk you in there and then I will let you have five minutes with Kate. You got that?" James asks.

"Five minutes is so stingy, but I'll take it. Let's go. Take me to see Kate," Gramps says, and then he puts his hand out so James can take it. They walk hand in hand down the hall toward Mom's room.

All I can do is hope that Gramps doesn't decide to pick on Mom about something dumb.

After nearly eight minutes, I cannot just sit there anymore. I start walking toward Mom's room.

Mom is awake, but she looks calm. She has a few things attached to her veins, but she is totally focused on Gramps. He is holding her hand and telling her a story. She has a small smile on her lips. James has his head in his hands on the other side of the bed. I stand there for a moment. I don't want to intrude and I don't want to make her nervous, but I want to see her. I want her to see me.

"Mommy," I say in a soft voice. I stand over Gramps, who is still going on. My mom turns to me and her smile deepens.

"How are you?" I ask.

She nods and I can tell that she is trying her best to stay calm.

Gramps is going on about a woman named Sylvia, who challenged him to a card game. Mom is not really listening, but she is content just to focus on the sound of his voice. When Gramps is telling one of his stories, his voice can be soothing.

I walk over to James.

He looks at me and tries his best to smile.

After a few minutes, a nurse comes into the room and kicks us all out. It's time to assess the situation and decide if it's time to induce Mom's labor.

We go back to the waiting room. Seeing Mom has made me feel a little better. Gramps is in good spirits, still going on about Sylvia and the card game. I decide to take out the turkey sandwich and Gramps is more than happy to wolf down his half.

I see some white coats go into Mom's room. I don't point this out to James, because he looks like he may pass out as it is. I try to breathe. I tell myself that this will all turn out all right. I can remember several months ago, when I was here at this very hospital. Mom was so helpful. I was scared out of my mind, but she calmed me. She rubbed my shoulders and told me that it would all work out and it did. I'm all right.

Mom has to be all right. That's all there is to it.

A half hour crawls by before the door to Mom's room opens. One nurse and one doctor exit and walk toward us. James sees them and practically lunges at them in search of information.

"Do you have news?" James asks.

Poor guy. He's totally freaking. I wish I could help him, but I've got my own worries to contend with. What if Mom isn't all right? What if the baby doesn't come through? What's going to happen to me?

Dr. Kankro introduces himself. He is a man in his late sixties. He's tall and thin with glasses and a white mustache. He smiles and takes a minute to take us all in. He sees me, the nervous teenage daughter, Gramps, the jolly old geezer, and James, the nervous new husband who is about to be a father for the first time.

"Kate is getting prepped for surgery right now. We are going to do an emergency C-section. We just can't afford to wait any longer because the baby is starting to show signs of distress."

I hear James gasp. He covers his mouth. The word emergency is so difficult.

"Under ordinary circumstances, we would have you in the operating room, but at this time, Mr. Breckinridge, we feel that it is in Kate's best interest not to have you in the operating room.

Therefore, you may all go into Kate's room and wish her a speedy delivery. The nurse will be coming around for her in about fifteen minutes."

"I can't be in the operating room with her?" James is asking. "That's not a good sign."

"Well, it's just a precaution. We don't want to expose Kate to any risk of infection. The surgery should take about an hour. When the baby is born, we will come for you, and you will be able to take the baby to Kate. Relax, Mr. Breckinridge. Kate's in good hands."

James nods.

"What do you mean the baby is starting to show signs of distress?" I ask.

"According to the fetal monitor, her blood pressure is starting to rise. It's nothing we're terribly concerned about. This is probably just her way of saying, 'Let me out!'" says Dr. Kankro.

Then he smiles and then walks to the nurse's station, where he is being pulled in several directions.

I don't know what to do with myself.

Gramps has stopped talking about Sylvia the card shark, and he is just staring into space. James is busily texting someone.

I go to Mom. She is awake, but woozy. She looks stoned. I smile at her and run my hands through her dark hair.

"You have to be a big girl, Lacey. Take care of everything until I'm all right." I nod. I feel hot tears filling my eyes. I don't want her to see me cry.

"Of course, I'll take care of things, Mom. No worries."

"Make sure James is all right. I know he's having a hard time. Help him along," she says. "He's a worry wart."

Mom smiles.

"Don't worry about a thing! Just go have that little sister of mine." I try to smile. I kiss her cheeks and her lips. I squeeze her hand.

As I leave the room, Gramps goes in. I make my way down the hall. Suddenly, I see a long, lean figure dressed all in black, coming off the elevator. It's Becky. I rush toward her and she takes me in her arms. Becky smells of onions, garlic, and lemon soap. I close my eyes and get lost in her.

CHAPTER THREE

Hello Daisy Rose

A few hours later, Daisy is born. She is the prettiest newborn baby in the whole nursery. She has a halo of reddish-brown hair, big blue eyes, and the cutest red lips. First, she is taken to her father, who is so excited to meet her. James is crying uncontrollably. Then it is my turn. I kiss Daisy once on the head and twice on the cheek. I welcome her into the world and promise her that I will be the best big sister anyone could want. Unfortunately, Mom is not able to meet Daisy right away. She is whisked off to the intensive care unit because of the preeclampsia. The first few hours of Daisy's life are scary for all of us, but not because of Daisy. She is absolutely fine. Mom is not doing well, and the doctors are concerned that she might have a seizure. When I see her, she does not look anything like my mother. She has just given birth, but she looks larger and puffier than before. Her face is distorted. She is not conscious. There are all sorts of machines attached to her. When Gramps comes into her room and sees her, he actually loses his footing and falls over. Thank goodness he falls into James instead of the hard floor, where he could have broken a bone or five.

James sits with Mom for the next few hours. Gramps sits outside the nursery and gazes at the new girl in his life. A friendly nurse sets him up with a chair, so he can relax. And I go to the hospital chapel and pray for the first time in my life. I don't exactly pray a specific prayer, but I talk to God. I tell him that we have come so far, and that we are finally at the point where we can actually be a family. I tell him that I will do whatever it takes to be strong and good. I promise to be the best daughter if he will just make Mom well again. Please let her wake up and see Daisy and get better. I sit in the chapel for at least an hour. It is peaceful and spiritual and I feel close to something I never knew before.

The door opens and Becky is standing there.

"Well, here you are, Lace. I was looking all over for you!" she says.

"What is it? Is it Mom?" I ask. Please don't let it be bad. Please.

"Yes, it's Kate. The doctors came by the waiting room to look for you. They said that her pressure is coming down, the swelling is coming down. They said it's a really good sign."

"Oh God!" I cry out. "Thank you. He listened."

Becky comes and sits next to me. "Who listened?"

"God. He really exists!" I say.

"Um, yea, Lace. But, who said God is a he? How could God be a he? God has to be a she. Think about it!" she says.

"I was praying for the first time in my life, Becky. I was making all kinds of deals with God. I told him that if he protected my family, I would be the best possible person," I say.

"That's great. Really great," says Becky. She puts her hand on my back. "But God is a she not a he?"

I give Becky a blank stare. "Whatever!" I say. "I talked to God." And then we laugh.

I grab Becky's hand and we go have another look at Daisy.

Mom and Daisy stay in the hospital for eight long days. In that time, Mom's swelling gradually disappears. Mom begins to feel like herself and look like herself, but it is a difficult journey. The nurses make her get up and walk but her body does not feel ready. She is weak, but holding Daisy gives her strength. James and I are getting the house ready for the baby. The day before Mom and Daisy come home, some teachers from Mom's school stop by with casseroles, cakes, and baby gifts.

Bringing Mom and Daisy home is sweet. At first, everything is wonderful. The baby is the sweetest thing ever and every minute is an opportunity to pull out my phone and snap a picture. It's so good to see that Mom no longer looks like a human balloon. She is smiling and happy and full of mirth. When Daisy cries, Mom rushes to her. She puts her on her breast, or sings or dances around with her. James is really good about changing diapers. I love waking up and holding my sister. I guess it is the honeymoon phase, because after a while, hysteria sets in. We are all exhausted. It seems Daisy likes to stay up during the nights and sleep during the days.

Daisy also has a lot of painful gas. It makes her not just cry, but wail. I have a hard time getting up for school because I am so tired in the mornings. James is so tired, that one day he goes to work wearing two different sneakers. Mom says she feels like she is losing her mind.

Sometimes two days pass before she can shower. She says she has no idea how she will ever go back to work, which is supposed to happen in a few months.

James' parents postpone their trip to meet Daisy until Christmas. That's a bummer because I was hoping to get a break and let them take my babysitting shifts. There are many days where Daisy just wants to sleep, but we all have to poke her gently and talk to her and make her stay awake, so that she'll be tired at night. We sometimes have to let her just cry herself to sleep during the night, even though it's hard to listen to the cries. One night I find Mom sitting on the floor sobbing in the nursery.

She says she is so tired she can't think straight.

I pick up Gramps once a week and he spends the night with us. During that time, Gramps holds Daisy and talks to her about all kinds of nonsense. Mom uses the time to take a shower, cook a meal, or go out for a walk. Gramps tells us that this is just a period of adjustment and that things will get better once Daisy realizes that only vampires stay up at night.

One Saturday, Becky comes over and orders us all to take a nap. She takes Daisy into the nursery and plays music for her. She talks to my little sister about her feelings toward Hoff. Daisy seems entertained. After two hours, Mom wakes up refreshed and happy. She kisses Becky and tells her how much she loves her. Becky burps, and Mom doesn't even roll her eyes.

All the while, Christmas is coming. The tree is up and presents are making their way under it. Mom and James decide to have Christmas dinner catered, which I think is the best idea, because, really, who wants to cook? We definitely want to eat, but we don't have the time to prepare the food ourselves. Not with little Miss Daisy filling our every waking moment. We are excited about meeting James' parents, who will arrive Christmas morning. James's mother is into scrapbooking and knitting, and his dad is a retired dentist. It should be interesting, and I'm wondering how Gramps will fit into the equation. The house is starting to look colorful and fancy, like a big gift from Santa.

Thoughts of Jack begin to bombard my head.

We have all sorts of sweaters, hats, and sleepers that read *Baby's First Christmas*. James hangs holiday lights. He also sets up a team of tacky reindeer in the front yard. We've had just a few snow showers, but the air is cold and it feels like it could snow at any time. Everything in the house is glowing and glistening, including Mom's tacky collection of Christmas snow globes. Personalized stockings are hung by the fireplace. These arrived a few days ago from Arlene, James' mom. There's *James*,

Kate, *Lacey*, *Daisy*, and even one for *Gramps*. This is all so exciting for me. In the past, Mom went through the motions, but we never had a Christmas like this before. Christmas was a chore. It was reminder that she had to do it all alone. It was as if someone was ordering her to be happy and love Christmas, but she didn't want to lift her head up from her pillow. She went through the motions on my account, but she never truly enjoyed herself. But this year is different. Every time I walk into the house, I get a whiff of the pine from the tree. It's so magical. Best time of year ever!

Thoughts of Jack begin to bombard my head.

I have been very disciplined this last month. I have kept my mind clear of Jack thoughts for the most part. At bedtime, I would allow myself five minutes to reflect on my time with Jack. During those moments, I might think about how it felt to kiss him, or I might replay one of our dates.

And because I have not spent too much time thinking Jack thoughts, I have managed to ace my mid-terms, even math, miracle of miracles, and, now, I am ready to concentrate on Jack. I am imagining his touch and his scent. I am allowing myself to fall in love all over again. I can't fight this feeling. It's too strong.

On Christmas Eve Day, Mom is crying about how ugly she is. Say what? It comes out of nowhere. One minute she is nursing the baby, and the next she is crying. James says this is all due to hormones. I don't know what to think. It's difficult seeing her sobbing, especially now that everything is all right. She is no longer swollen like a human balloon, and Daisy is doing really well.

I try to tell Mom that she is far from ugly. I try to make her laugh by showing her pictures of people who are really ugly. James spends hours complimenting her, but none of it seems to have an impact. I tell her that Christmas is coming and that it is such a beautiful time of year. That doesn't do it. She says the tree makes her happy and she loves Daisy and me and James, but she just feels so unattractive. When I tell her that beauty comes from the inside, she throws her pillow at me.

Then I have an idea. Becky has an aunt who works at Glamour and Glitz in the mall. She's a really sweet lady, and Becky says she's always up to doing my hair. I ask Becky if her Aunt would be willing to give Mom a total makeover. I explain all the circumstances about how Mom is tripping about how ugly she has become. Becky loves the idea. Sure enough, Mom thinks it's a great idea. She smiles at the thought of a new look.

"Can she fix me, Lace?" Mom asks.

"I don't think you need fixing. I think you're perfect. You just need a lift," I say. "A face lift!" Mom quips.

"Mom, stop, you're beautiful. Now you're just fishing."

And I really mean what I say. Mom is a very pretty woman. She's got big eyes and dark, long lashes. Her skin is smooth and white as porcelain. If anything, she just needs something to freshen her look. She needs a little rosy in her cheeks, a little shine in her hair, and then she will be golden again.

Mom is busy getting ready for her 3:00 Glamour and Glitz appointment.

"I hope they can do my nails, too," she says, as she slips out of her sweats. I nod and smile at her. I am holding a sleeping baby girl.

Sometimes, when Daisy is in my arms it feels too weird for words. I look down at her, and I think, what if what happened to me ended differently? What if the little bundle in my arms was really my bundle and I had to be responsible for it? What would happen then? What if Mom was the one who lost the baby, and I was the one who had the baby? These thoughts can really do a number on me. I love Daisy so much. If she was my baby, I would love her, but would I be able to give her what she needed? No way. And what about Jack in all this? It's wrong not to tell him about what happened to me. I must tell him about this. But it's so hard for me to talk to anyone about this. Whenever Mom brings it up, I feel like I am going to choke.

Mom has on a pair of pre-pregnancy jeans that are a little tight, but not too bad, and a red long sleeved tunic shirt. She is wearing my Frye boots, and she's asking me if she looks all right. But I am busy wrapped up in my thoughts. What if the baby was born and it looked like Jack? What if Jack was with someone else and I had his baby? Would he want to take the baby and raise it with the other person?

"Really? Come back to the planet, Lace!" Mom sounds angry. I am brought back into reality.

"You look pretty, Mom. Really good." I say and give her a thumb's up. "You all right? Where did you just go?" she asks.

"To the dark center of Lacey's world," I answer. Mom rolls her eyes.

"Are you sure you can do this, Lace?" she asks.

"Of course, I'm done with mid-terms and I am all yours. James is picking up Gramps in a little while. I'm fine. Take your time," I say. "This will be nice for Daisy and me. Some sister time where we can talk about how weird our mom is!"

Mom smiles. She's so excited to be getting out of the house.

"Don't tell her about me before I was the me I am now," says Mom. "What?" I ask.

"You know. She doesn't have to know what a grouchy person I was in the past," pleads Mom.

"Mom," I say.

"What? I know I was."

"Let's just hold off on that chapter," I say. Mom nods.

"Good idea," she says. "This is going to be so much fun," she says. "Now if she wakes up, I have some breast milk in the freezer."

I nod.

"It's all good. Go, Mom. Get beautiful."

Mom kisses me on the head and then takes a minute to stare at her sleeping angel, who is dressed in a red velvet jumper. The red matches the color of her lips.

Mom leaves and a little while later, James leaves to pick up Gramps and then go to the store to pick up some dinner for tonight. I am on the couch with Daisy in my arms and a cup of coffee by my side. Ahhh, a quiet moment before all the holiday craziness begins.

I close my eyes and can feel myself drifting off. A nap will be good. I settle into the couch, just as the doorbell rings. I consider not getting it, but then I figure, what if it's a Christmas package? I get up slowly, so as not to wake my sleeping sister, who is in my arms. I get to the front door, and open it. There. In front of my eyes. He. Jack. Standing there. His eyes are curious. He's looking confused. He's looking horrified. He's carrying two Starbucks coffees in a cardboard tray. He's also holding a huge grocery bag.

"Jack?"

"Lacey?"

I smile. Jack. He's so gorgeous.

"Come in," I say, and I hold open the screen door. Jack stands frozen.

"Who is that?" Jack asks, pointing to the baby. "I have Daisy," I say.

Jack comes into the house, but the color is gone from his face.

"I don't understand. Where does she come from?" he asks. "Is she?"

Jack looks like he might pass out.

"She's my sister!" I smile brightly.

"Your sister?" Jack breaks into a wide grin. "Your mom and James had a baby?" I nod.

"Yep. They did. James and Mom got married."

"That's awesome."

"It's good to see you," I say.

"I didn't call. I thought I'd just come by. That way, you had no choice but to see me."

"I've been looking forward to it every day since we last saw each other," I confess.

"Really?" he asks. "Really," I answer.

We stand there together taking it all in.

I lead Jack into the kitchen and tell him to put his stuff on the table. Then I place Daisy in his arms. Just as I thought, Jack immediately takes to the baby. He looks comfortable holding a baby. He holds her with confidence. He is sweet and loving.

"She looks like you, Lace. What a Christmas for you guys, huh?" he says. I nod. "It's good to see you, Jack," I say, because it is.

If Daisy wasn't in his arms right now, I would be. "What did you bring, Jack?"

"Coffee for us. Decaf. And the bag is filled with chicken wings, meatballs, and cheese sticks from the deli. Figured if you guys had company, it's a great thing to have in the fridge."

"Whoa, my mom is going to love you."

"Where is everyone?" Jack asks.

"It's just us and Daisy. Mom is at the salon, and James is taking care of errands and picking up Gramps."

Gramps!" exclaims Jack. "How is he? How does he like Daisy?"

"He loves her. It's just been the best thing for him. For everyone." We stand there and look at each other.

My hands are shaking.

"When you first came to the door, I thought, I thought the baby was yours." I nod. Oh God.

"I can understand."

"It's so good to see you," he says. "It's been so long."

"I didn't expect to see you until tomorrow. I thought tomorrow Jack will call and I will see him. This is a major surprise. Major surprise," I say. "Let's put Daisy in her crib. Follow me."

I feel so anxious. I just want to jump on top of Jack. We walk into the nursery and Jack is going on about what a great job James has done with the house.

"It's hard to believe it's the same place, Lace."

I watch Jack, as he gently places Daisy in her crib. He smiles at her. Then he looks at me.

He has a serious expression. He takes off his parka and I take it and put it on the rocking chair next to the crib. Jack is wearing a dark brown cashmere sweater, jeans, and work boots. His hair is short and brown with flecks of gold. His skin is smooth and tan. His lips are perfect.

"You look beautiful," he says. "Really? I just woke up," I say.

My hair feels so messy. I am wearing skinny jeans, slippers, and a tight purple sweater. I don't think this would be my first outfit choice if I knew Jack was coming over, but it certainly is not my last choice.

He comes toward me and I can smell the cinnamon-ocean mix. I am intoxicated by him. His lips slowly come to mine. What am I doing? Should I let this happen? Will I get hurt again? But how can I resist this guy, this wonderful guy, who makes me feel like I am standing on the edge of a cliff, and I am about to bungee jump. This is the person who makes me feel special and beautiful and funny. This is my person. My match. The kiss is long and slow and deep. It's everything I thought it would be and more.

In seconds, I have wrapped my arms around his neck. My fingers are making their way through his hair. I am so absorbed in his kiss, I can't help but moan and whisper his name.

He responds to that, and I am afraid that if we don't stop, we will be naked very soon. I pull away gently, slowly.

"Missed me?" he asks, with a smirk.

It's the perfect icebreaker and we both laugh.

We go to the family room. It's the new room that James has built. It's got green walls, a skylight, soft brown leather couches, a large rustic wooden coffee table and bright orange

accents. It's the happy room. Jack admires it and stands around taking it all in. Then he goes to the kitchen to get our coffees. I take a second to check myself in the bathroom mirror. I quickly put on some eyeliner, mascara, lips gloss, and a spritz of perfume.

Jack is on the couch drinking his coffee and smiling. "What did you do? You look so pretty!" he says.

I just blush.

"Come here. It's been like forever." His expression becomes serious. I sit close to him and take a sip of my coffee.

"Perfect!" I say. "Are you back for good?" I ask trying not to act like my life depends on his response.

He nods.

"I am. I'm a different person." I nod.

"I guess I am, too."

"I'll bet. Your life has really changed. What's it like? Do you have a good relationship with James?"

"He's awesome! Nicest guy. And my mom is great. Who knew?" I say. Jack laughs out loud. "I did."

"You did, didn't you?" Jack nods.

"It's been a long ride. Mom was sick after she had the baby. She was in the hospital for almost two weeks. Her entire body was swollen. It was so scary."

Jack is all ears and all eyes on me. One of the things I love about him.

"That must have been terrible for you and James. I wish I could have helped you."

I'm about to go on and tell him about how I ended up in the hospital chapel because I think he'd like to hear that, but the next thing I know, Jack has moved in for another irresistible kiss.

I don't understand why I am so drawn to this boy. I want him so badly, despite all the pain and the loneliness I've suffered as a result of my feelings for him. I just want his body against mine.

How can that be wrong? His tongue is getting reacquainted with my neck. I am writhing in passion for this guy. It's even more intense than I remembered. I feel like I am on a rollercoaster.

He is whispering to me about how he's missed me, how he's thought about me, and how he wants to make it all up to me. He's got plans and ideas and he hopes that I will give him the chance to show his true colors. And just then, in the middle of this beautiful moment, I hear a cry. A loud cry that turns into a wail.

"Sounds like someone is hungry!" Jack says. We both laugh.

Jack gets up and holds out his hand to me. "Let's go see what that girl wants," he says.

Daisy is screaming her head off. Jack is a bit thrown by it. He is running his hands in his hair. I pick her up and change her diaper, which is so gross. Words cannot describe it. I tell Jack to step out of the room while I do the dirty deed.

Then I get a bottle and we head to the couch. The hysterical cries have stopped, but the hungry cry is happening. I give Daisy the bottle and then there is quiet. Bliss. But Daisy is so thirsty and hungry, we can hear her gulping.

"Is that her?" Jack asks.

"Yep. A little hungry, there, huh?" I ask Daisy. Is that normal?" Jack asks, looking horrified. I laugh. Then he laughs.

"What is normal?" I say, in a peculiar voice, and roll my eyes.

Then the gulping stops. Jack and I are watching Daisy intently. What is she going to do next? And then, there it is. Daisy makes this earth shattering burp. How could something so little make something so big?

"Does she remind you of Becky, or what?" Jack asks. Then we both burst out laughing.

Jack has his arm around me. For a minute, I think this could be our baby. This is freaky thinking and I need to stop it. It's just that, if this were my baby, I mean, mine and Jack's baby, there would be some good moments, like this one. There would be times when we would just be able to kick back and look at our kid and think, 'Wow, we did this.' But I know this is a dangerous thought and I should talk to Jack about it all. He would want to know how this could have happened. We used a condom every time. I know that we did, but who knows what happened to it? I have got to tuck these thoughts away, because I can't handle them. Too sad. Too loaded with anxiety.

"What do you want for Christmas, Lace?" Jack asks in a quiet tone.

I welcome the change of subject from the anxious thoughts that are dancing in my head. I want. I want Jack back in my life. I want everything to be good again.

I shake my head because I don't know what to say. I look up at Jack. "What do you want?" I ask.

"You. But I want to keep on the right road. It's different being sober. Don't get me wrong, it's the right path for me, but it's really hard, sometimes. It's all about making choices. You can't just cruise. Everything has to be part of a plan."

I had no idea. I thought you just stop drinking and while it may be hard because drinking for Jack is as natural as Becky burping, I didn't really think about how complicated it is to stop.

"What was Uncle Aiden like?" I ask.

"Brutal. He's a big, tough dude. He never lets me off the hook. I always have to have a plan, a purpose. But he's also a good guy. When I follow what he says, he's the nicest guy."

Jack seems older. His voice is deeper. I study his hands. The skin is rough and chapped by the knuckles, but they are the hands that I love.

"What else have you been doing?"

"Going to high school out in California was really odd. I never really adjusted to it. Never made friends. Just studied. Whenever I wasn't at school, I was building decks and patios with Aiden. Hard work, but I made a load of cash. Working helped to pass the time." I nod.

"I never thought that I would see you again. I thought you were in California for good. When I saw you at Thanksgiving, I just couldn't believe that you would be coming back," I say.

Daisy is finished with her bottle. She looks up at us and makes a funny face.

"There was no way I was staying in California if I had a chance to be with you," says Jack. "Really?" I ask.

"Are you kidding me, Lace? I did whatever I could do to make my way back to you."

Jack kisses me. I close my eyes. I am not dreaming. What did I do to deserve this attention from this beautiful guy? I don't know if Jack can see my tears. I just want to hold this boy until the end of my life.

Mom comes home first. She is calling my name, as she walks through the house. "In the family room, Mom," I call out.

Mom comes in and she's got big, bright red hair down to her shoulders. She's all made up and her nails have become magically long and dark red. This is a very different look for my mom, who has never dyed her hair before. Mom, with her bright red hair looks like that cartoon character Kim Possible!

I am staring. Mom is staring at Jack, and Jack is walking toward her to shake her hand and tell her how well she looks and what a beautiful girl Daisy is. Jack is such a natural when it comes to dealing with people.

"Jack! How are you? It's good to see you? I didn't know you were in town," she says. My mom gives Jack a kiss on the cheek.

"Actually, I'm back. For good," Jack says.

My mom is processing that. I know she is wondering if that is really best for me. I try to change the subject.

"Who are you, and what have you done with my mom?" I say. "You look so glam."

That is as good as my compliment can get at this moment. I am not really sure if I like this look on my mom. It's too radically different. But Daisy hears her mommy and cries out for her. Mom comes toward me and picks up Daisy.

Mom is talking baby talk to Daisy.

"What's in the big bag on the table?" she asks. "Jack brought over some food," I say.

"Bless you, Jack. I haven't cooked in the last two months," she says. "And I don't plan on cooking for at least another two months."

Jack laughs.

"I can imagine. You've been busy," he says.

"Well, I know one person who is going to be really happy to see you," Mom says. "Oh yeah," asks Jack. "Who is that?"

"Gramps, of course," Mom says.

I excuse myself for a minute to go to the bathroom. As I leave, I can hear my mother asking Jack about California and how he is feeling. By the time I return, Jack is telling Mom all about his experience with Uncle Aiden. I almost feel like I am walking in on a private conversation. Mom is gentle and really sweet to Jack. She explains that she's genuinely happy for him that he is in control of his life now.

Mom suggests that we heat up some of the snacks that Jack brought so that by the time Gramps and James arrive, they will be nice and hot.

Since they look so comfortable talking to each other, I offer to do it by myself, but Jack stands and says he'll help. Mom stays on the couch with Daisy.

Gramps comes into the house wearing a Santa hat, and saying "ho, ho, ho." He is wearing a red turtle neck and black wool pants. He doesn't look anything like Santa, but he could definitely pass for an elf. He is so cute. I just laugh.

He is holding Rosey-O, a tiny mutt with a big bark. James is carrying Gramps' bag and a shopping bag from Trader Joes.

"Well, look who it is? Hello, Jack. Merry Christmas!" say James.

James looks at me for a sign. Is this something I want? Am I OK with Jack being here? I smile to show that it's all good.

"Merry Christmas, James. Good to see you, and congratulations on your beautiful baby," Jack says, shaking James' hand.

Gramps looks at Jack and walks toward him.

"How are you, kid? Happy Christmas! Have you been a good boy?"

"Gramps, it's great to see you. And who is this?" Jack asks.

"Meet Rosey-O. Isn't she the sweetest, cutest puppy in the world?" I say, and then I pick her up. Jack is petting her and playing with her. Rosey-O is teeny tiny and so cute. She is wearing a pair of red antlers. Too cute for words.

"Are you home for good, Jack?" James asks. "I think so, James. I hope so."

James nods and offers Jack a soda. I explain that we have snacks in the oven from Jack. Mom comes into the kitchen carrying Daisy, who is wearing a new outfit of black velvet with tiny daisies on it.

"Mom, Daisy's outfit is so sweet," I say.

James and Gramps look at Mom. She doesn't look like herself. Her hair is bright red. "What happened to you?" ask Gramps.

"A new look? It's so pretty, Kate. You are going to turn heads with that red hair. I love it," James says. He is such a peace maker, but James might be going a little overboard about Mom's new look. He is so protective of her feelings.

"Your hair is fire engine red, Kate! What's the matter with you? You trying to stop traffic? Geez," says Gramps. "You trying to give me a heart attack?"

"It's beautiful. I've always loved red hair," James says.

He goes over to Mom and kisses her on the lips. Then he kisses Daisy on the head. "I guess I'll have to get used to it, Red," says Gramps, as he sits at the table.

Everyone in the room nods. Mom smiles.

"It's not like I have a choice," Gramps quips. "Merry Christmas, Red!" he says to Mom. Gramps goes over to his littlest granddaughter and starts making funny faces and silly noises.

Something about this gathering is just so right. Christmas is wrapped around us like a pretty gold ribbon. Even the wails from hungry Daisy can't ruin my joyful feeling.

Later that night, I am getting settled into the couch in the family room. Gramps has my room, which is fine with me, because in exchange for the use of my room, he has given me Rosey-O for the night. Mom comes in to see me. Against the white of her nightgown, her red hair is definitely a little scary.

"Mom, what's up?" I ask.

She sits at my feet and rests her hand on my leg.

"To tell you the truth, Lace, I was trying to get your hair, not this look."

"Did you ask for red highlights?" I ask.

"No. I said, 'make it red.'"

Mom and I laugh. It's a big hearty laugh. "Highlights, Mom," I say. "Highlights." And then we are quiet.

"Did you know he was coming back, Lace?" she asks. I nod. "Jack?"

"No, Santa Claus!" I smile.

"I ran into him a few days before Daisy was born. I was going to tell you, but things were so tense, and I just didn't want to stress you with it. He told me he was coming back for good at Christmas."

Mom looks at me.

"And how do you feel about that? I mean, don't get me wrong, he is such a nice kid. Sweet, smart, and really cute."

"Are you attracted to Jack, Mom?" I ask, of course, I'm joking. I'm just trying to keep the mood light.

"Are you kidding? He's adorable!" I smile. Jack *is* so cute.

"Well, I'm a little nervous. I know it won't be easy. He is a senior now, and he's got to buckle down if he wants to get into a good college," I say.

"But, you did tell him all the details, right? Did you tell him you were pregnant?" Oh God. There it is. The elephant in the room. I was pregnant. With Jack's baby. I don't say anything. I just look down at the floor.

"I didn't think you did," Mom says.

"Mom, it's just too much right now. I don't want to go there," I say.

"I know. But, at some point, I think he has a right to know. Especially, if the two of you are going to have a relationship. I can understand why you haven't said anything now with the holidays and all. Just make sure you tell him. You want to keep things open and honest. That's key to a perfect relationship."

I look at mom. Something is very odd.

"Mom, what is going on? How come you've got wet patches on your boobs? What does that mean?"

"It means, somewhere in this house, there is a monster baby who is hungry!" Mom says with a hearty laugh.

And just then, James comes into the room. He's dressed in flannel pajama bottoms and a white T-shirt. He's carrying his daughter in his arms.

"Special delivery," he says.

Mom laughs. Then she takes the baby from James and she nurses Daisy. James sits down and asks if anyone wants anything to eat, even though it's well after eleven.

"I wouldn't mind a little something," Mom says.

"I could go for a little something, too," I say, and smile at James. James gets up and says he's got just the thing.

In a few minutes he's back with a tray of cheese, crackers, leftover chicken wings, and pieces of celery. He also has a pitcher of water and some cups.

"What a perfect snack!" I say.

As James is reminding Mom that she has to make sure that she drinks enough water so that she makes enough milk for Daisy, I am feeding Rosey-O little bits of cracker.

James is munching on a chicken wing.

"Nice guy, that Jack. I really like him, Lace."

"We've been discussing that," Mom says. "And?" asks James, reaching for another wing.

"Well, it looks like Lacey knew that he was coming back for good. She ran into him just before

the baby was born. She didn't tell us because she didn't want to add to the stress. I just hope Jack can handle it all," Mom says.

"It's not easy to quit drinking," James, says. "I respect the guy for trying." James takes a big gulp of water. He leans back on the couch and looks down.

"My dad drank for years. He was a nasty drunk. He doesn't drink anymore, but it took a long time for him to be able to really give it up."

"Did you have problems with drinking?" I ask.

"No. I drink a few beers here and there, but it's never been like it is with my dad. He tried many times to give it up. He's a smart man. He was a successful dentist. But when it came to drinking, the habit was bigger than he was."

I can tell Mom has mixed feelings about meeting James' parents tomorrow.

We are all quiet for a while. Rosey-O settles herself on my chest under the blanket.

"Do you think your parents will like my hair, James?" Mom picks up a few strands of fire engine red and studies them.

"Probably not," says James. "Definitely not." Then they both burst out laughing.

CHAPTER FOUR

Christmas Is Upon Us

Christmas Day starts out crazy. I get a wake-up call from Mason. He says, "Merry Christmas." I say it back, and then he says, "So, did you see him?"

Now I am thinking that Mason needs to mind his own beeswax. This is ridiculous. "Yes, I saw him."

"Well, are you back together or what?"

The nerve of this guy. Rosey-O wants the phone, so I give it to her. She is licking it and I can hear Mason say, "Hello? Hello? Lacey? Are you there?"

After a minute or so, I take back the phone and say, "Have a great holiday, Mase." Then I hang up. Move on, Mason. I'm never going to be attracted to you. Not in a million years. If you are not satisfied with my friendship than you can just get out. I have enough on my plate. It's not even 8:30 in the morning, and that freak is asking me if I am back together with Jack.

Why does everyone care so much about me and Jack? I got a few phone calls from August last week saying that she had heard that Jack was coming home for Christmas and staying home. She wanted to know if I knew this news, if I was prepared for it, and what my strategy was going to be to try to win him back. Gee, can you believe some people? I got really pissed at her, but I tried not to show it. I told her I already knew that, and that I had already seen Jack at Thanksgiving.

She was all annoyed that she hadn't heard anything about this. Get a life, bitch!

I am just going to have the best possible Christmas today. There's a new baby in the house, and Mom has her man, and I've got Gramps and Rosey-O, and Jack will be joining us for dessert. When Mom asked Jack over for Christmas dinner, I was hoping that he would say that his parents are expecting him for dinner. I mean, don't get me wrong, I want to see him and be with him in the worst way, but I would also like to relax today. I just want to be free and easy, not wear makeup, walk around in sweats, and not shower until dinnertime. I just want to feel at home and sit in the living room and gaze at the tree, and not worry that my hair isn't perfect. Isn't that what Christmas is really about? Not having anyone look at you and tell you that you have bags under your eyes or a zit on your chin. Ahhh, Christmas.

But now, suddenly, James and Mom are in my face, and they are in panic mode. I've got to get up and clean the room, fix breakfast for Gramps, and pick up the food from the caterer because James' parents will be here in a few hours.

But what about my Christmas? And, I forgot about Rosey-O. I'm sure she needs to be taken out. That's the end of my relaxed vision of Christmas. Oh well. It's still Christmas, and that's got to put a smile on your face.

"Merry Christmas," I say, as I get up and start my chores. When I walk out of the family room, and down the hall to the bathroom, I catch a glimpse of the living room. The tree looks so pretty, and there are so many presents underneath it.

"Hey," I say. Those presents weren't there last night."

I mean, there were a few presents there last night, but nothing like this.

Mom laughs and James smiles. James. I knew he would love Christmas. He's wearing a big cheesy Christmas sweater and green slacks.

"Santa came!" he says. "He did not!" I say. "Oh yes he did!"

"He did not!" I say with a smile.

Mom walks past me and says, "Yes, he did. And, he even ate the cookies we left for him."

All right. I can play along. After all, this *is* what it's all about. For the next I-don't-know-how many Christmases, it will all be about Santa and the reindeer. Daisy is in for some fun. But of course, for this Christmas, it wouldn't matter to her if Santa skipped out of town. She only knows milk, crying, and sleeping. But all that will change soon enough.

I go to the bathroom to wash up, put my hair in braids, and get dressed in sweats and a flannel shirt. Then I head to the kitchen to make a plate of scrambled eggs and a cup of coffee for Gramps.

When Gramps comes out of the bathroom, I walk toward him.

Breakfast is on the table, Gramps."

"Is that my little angel?" Gramps asks. "Yes. It's me."

He looks so cute in his plaid pajamas. I take his hand and walk him to the table. He sits and begins to eat.

"Not bad, Lace. I can tell you didn't learn to make eggs from your mom. She can't make eggs to save her life," Gramps says, sticking a big forkful of fluffy eggs in his mouth. "That's good."

"Merry Christmas, Gramps," I say.

I lean in and give him a kiss on the cheek. He smiles.

"Wait 'til you see what I got you for Christmas." Gramps can't wait to give me my present. He's all excited about it.

"I can't wait. But remember, Gramps, it's not about the presents."

"Yeah, yeah, whatever you say, pretty girl," he says. "So, if I gave you a lump of coal, you'd be happy?" he asks. "See what I'm saying?"

"If it was from you, I would like it!"

Gramps laughs. He picks up his coffee cup and takes a nice, loud sip.

"Not bad, Lace. Not too strong. Your mom's coffee tastes like mud," he says. Poor Mom. In Gramps' eye, she can never do anything right.

I put on my hoodie and pick up Rosey.

"I'm going to take Rosey for a walk, Gramps."

"You really are an angel," he says. Then he holds out his hand to pet Rosey.

Do you want to come?" I ask.

I wait for an answer from Gramps, but I don't get one. He becomes interested in his plate and his coffee and he forgets that I am standing there. Mom says this is part of his getting old. He forgets a lot. I don't mind. He's still my Gramps.

So Rosey and I go for our walk without Gramps. No biggie.

After Rosey-O has been walked, I clean up the kitchen, and settle Gramps into the living room. Presents will not be opened until James' parents arrive. Gramps has the newspaper and Rosey-O for entertainment. Mom, James, and Daisy are at the airport.

Gramps has his head in the paper and Rosey on his lap.

"I am going out to pick up the food from the caterer," I shout. ramps does not respond.

I walk over to him and tap him on the shoulder. "What can I do for you?" he asks in a serious tone. "I'm going to pick up the food now!" I say.

"That's good, Rosey, I mean Lacey." He winks at me. I am off.

It is not a white Christmas. In fact, it is very mild outside. It's more like a fall day than a winter day. I head for my beat up old Saab, which James has fixed up for me, and head for the highway.

An hour later I am back with a huge roast beef, twenty-four fancy baked potatoes, a carrot soufflé, mixed vegetables, a salad, two loaves of bread, and three cakes. I set up all the food in the fridge so that it's ready for us to just toss in the oven.

Gramps has fallen asleep. What a surprise! While nobody else is around, I guess it is smart to take my shower now, do my hair, put on makeup and find a pretty outfit. So much for rolling around in my sweats. Maybe that's what I can do the day after Christmas.

I settle on a red sweater, a black skirt, black riding boots, and the necklace that Jack bought me. This is the first time I am wearing it since he left five months ago. I know that Jack will like it. I have set Jack's Starbucks mug and coffee under the tree. I am upset that I don't have a more substantial gift for him. I just didn't want to jinx it. Jack will understand.

Rosey-O is going nuts. Someone is at the door. Mom, Daisy, James, and James's parents are all here. I call out to Gramps to wake up. I head for the door all dressed up in my Christmas clothes. Mom smiles at me. James smiles and leads his parents into the house.

"This is Lacey," James says. "Lacey, this is my mom, Arlene and this is my dad, Breck."

I hold out my hand to shake Arlene's, but she throws her arms around me. She is a sweet lady with brown curly hair and big gray eyes. Her smile is James' smile. I immediately adore her.

"What a doll you are! You are so beautiful and James tells me that you are a brilliant writer!" she says.

"Well, I don't know if I would go that far! But, it's so nice to meet you, and congratulations on your beautiful granddaughter."

"What a love you are!" says Arlene. "Merry Christmas, dear, and may this be the beginning of a long and happy relationship."

Breck, however, is not so easy to win over. He's stiff. He politely extends his hand to me. "Hi, good to meet you!" I say.

Hc nods.

"Gramps, come and meet Breck," I say.

Gramps is tiny compared to Breck, but they are probably around the same age. "Merry Christmas," says Gramps.

"Merry Christmas," says Breck.

"What shall I call you?" Breck asks Gramps.

"I answer to almost anything. Gramps or John, I guess. My name is John. It sure is nice to meet you folks." Gramps has a big smile on, but Breck doesn't seem to know how to smile.

Gramps grabs hold of Arlene's hand and shakes it for a long time. She smiles. Breck just stands in the doorway.

Rosey-O jumps up on his leg, but Breck does not seem to like the canine attention. "Calm down, Rosey," I say.

"I hope she won't bother you. She's really just excited to meet you," I say to Breck. He practically ignores me.

Mom goes to put Daisy in her crib. James is putting on the coffee, and I am carrying the bags into the family room, where James' parents will be sleeping.

Arlene has a giant bag of gifts and she is busy placing them under the tree.

James has put on some Christmas music and he has opened a container of snowman cookies, which he is putting on a pretty red tray. Let's get this party started. Everyone is into it, except for Breck, who just stands at attention in front of the tree. Loser!

Arlene is going on about how lovely our house is and what a wonderful homemaker Mom must be. I am nodding and smiling. If opposites attract, than Arlene and Breck are made for each other. She is sweet as pie but he is as grouchy as can be.

"Dear," she says to me.

I am all ears with a big smile.

"I was wondering if I might have a word with you in private?" Arlene asks. "With me? Sure. Want to come in my room for a minute?" I ask.

She nods and follows me into my room. I have no idea what this is about. She comes into my room and closes the door.

"Is something wrong?" I ask.

Arlene smiles at me. Can this woman be so sweet, or is there another side to her? Am I about to experience another side to Arlene Breckinridge? I'm scared. I want my mommy.

"Dear, it's just that your Mom told me that she had her hair done yesterday and it's a little more than she expected."

I laugh.

"Just a bit. I think she was aiming for my reddish highlights, but instead she got all red," I explain.

"Yes. Yours is lovely."

The next thing I know, Arlene, who is a few inches taller than me, is circling my head and sticking her fingers in my hair. Weird. I can hear Rosey-O on the other side of my door. She's come to rescue me.

"Rosey is that you?" I ask. I open the door a bit, just so Rosey can enter. She rushes through the room and settles on a big pillow on the floor.

"Do you think it would be all right if I asked her if I could fix it?"

Arlene asks. Huh? What's this woman going on about? I make a confused expression.

"I am a hairdresser. Well, I was before I retired. I can run some dark brown into her hair and then we'd get just the nicest bit of red to stick around. What do you think?"

I laugh. "Mom would love that."

"She won't be offended? I don't want to offend her."

"No. Mom's not like that. She will love that you want to help her. And I can take you to the drug store tomorrow and you can buy what you need."

The next thing I know, Arlene is hugging me and telling me that she is so happy to be in my family.

"Shall we go and tell your mom about her hair and what I'd like to do?"

I nod. We walk into the nursery, where Daisy is sleeping and Mom is looking for something in Daisy's closet.

"Mom?" I say.

She turns and she is smiling and her face is so pretty. The hair, however, not so much. "Did you know that Arlene was, I mean is, a hairdresser?"

Mom looks at Arlene and smiles. "No."

"Well, guess what, Mom?" I say. "What's that?" she asks.

"Arlene has some ideas about how to get your hair to look more like mine with just the red highlights, instead of all the red."

Mom's smile droops. She looks at me and then at Arlene. "It's bad, isn't it?" she asks.

I don't say anything. I know Mom's too hormonal to deal with the truth. Arlene, however, is brave.

"Let's just say this: It's not doing anything for that fabulous face of yours," says Arlene.

Mom looks at me. Then she looks at Arlene. Then she cracks up. Arlene embraces her and they become instant best friends.

Without having to cook on Christmas Day, there is a lot more time for just hanging out. We are in the living room and we are about to open gifts, when the doorbell rings. It's Becky. She is dressed in black leggings, a black top, black heels, and a narrow red belt. To tell you the truth, I think she looks ridiculous. Too much black and the leggings with the heels? Come on! But she is full of Christmas cheer. She's brought me some perfume from Victoria's Secret. She also has some body cream for my mom, and for Daisy, she has a little stuffed giraffe. I give Becky my little gift and she stays for some coffee and cookies. Becky has no problem joining the party. She is lively and outgoing. She immediately loves Arlene, but when her burping starts, I can tell that Breck is put off by her. After a while, nobody tries to make conversation with Breck. He is just too grouchy. Gramps is smiling and laughing. Arlene is talking a mile a minute. Mom is giggling and squeezing James' knee, who is sitting on the couch next to her. Breck is just missing out on all this fun.

The doorbell rings again, and this time it's Olive and Rita, two teachers that Mom is friends with. They have brought Christmas cookies and a bottle of wine, and they are just here to say a quick hi, and to have a glance at the baby. With all the action going on, it isn't until about four in the afternoon, that we get to the presents. Everyone, with the exception of Breck, is opening presents, smiling, and laughing, and saying things like, "I love it!" and "How did you know?"

Arlene has knit me a sweater in the most beautiful shade of soft pink. It's gorgeous. Mom has bought me books, a scarf, leather gloves, and two phone chargers. James has given me a leather journal and a fancy pen. I even have a few gifts from my sister, Daisy. I've got new boots, two pairs of skinny jeans, a short leather jacket, and a pair of the softest, cuddliest pajamas. The sweetest gift of all, however, comes from Gramps. Wrapped in magazine paper, it is a framed photograph of the two of us. In it, I am about eight years old and I am sitting on the floor holding a doll, and Gramps is kneeling behind me with his arms around me. I've got this wicked smile on my face. Gramps looks exactly the same as he does in the photo, but with more gray hair.

I had forgotten who this girl was. In the photo. She is beautiful and smart and fun. She does not have the weight of the world on her. This girl loves to laugh. This girl is me.

As we all make our way to the dinner table, there is a big snag. Gramps is not happy about something. He tells Mom that there are not enough place settings. Mom is looking at the table, and then looking at the people in the room, and then looking at the table, and then the people in the room again.

"I don't see the problem, Dad. Daisy isn't sitting at the table."

"That's not the issue," Gramps pouts. He taps his foot on the ground and acts as if he is highly insulted.

James put his arm around Gramps and asks him what's wrong.

"What's wrong is that there is no place at the table for Rosey!" Gramps shouts. Everyone is quiet.

Is he kidding?

Gramps is serious. He's dead serious.

"She may be a dog, but she's family," he says.

Mom looks at James. James looks at me. I look at the floor. I don't want to say anything against Gramps after he's given me such a fine gift.

It's as if Rosey-O knows what we are talking about. She is quiet and looking up at us. Mom has a worried look on her face. She's wondering how she can fix this one.

James decides to take the lead.

"A minor adjustment," he says. He has his hands up in the air like he is about to conduct a piece of classical music. "Give me a minute to set a place next to Gramps for Rosey."

James takes a chair from the kitchen and puts a few pillows on top of it, so it's nice and plush and comfy for Rosey. Then he puts a small plastic plate on the table for Rosey.

"Please forgive us," he says to Gramps. "We forgot ourselves for a minute." Gramps nods. "Everyone makes mistakes," he says.

James is a really nice guy.

"How's this?" asks James.

Gramps walks to the table with Rosey in his arms. He places her on the chair and waits for a sign from her. She smells the area, circles a bit, and then sits waiting for her Christmas dinner. The seat meets her approval. We can all breathe a sigh of relief.

Gramps smiles.

"Rosey approves!" he says.

Everyone smiles tentatively at Gramps.

Is it normal to seat a dog at the table for Christmas dinner?

Dinner is awesome. The meat is tender and the potatoes are yummy. Everyone is going on about it, even Breck, who says the roast is cooked perfectly. I'm not sure if Mom and James told Arlene and Breck that the meal was catered, so I make sure not to say anything about the fact that the food is not homemade. Let them think Mom cooked it all herself.

Wine is served with the dinner, but only Mom and Arlene have some. James and Gramps are drinking beer, and Breck and I are having water. Daisy is in Mom's arms. She's awake, but she seems content to take in all the sights and sounds of the holiday.

Gramps is busy cutting the food in tiny pieces for his baby, Rosey-O. Every once in a while, I think I see Breck sneering at him. Arlene is describing the first second that she laid eyes on Daisy. She says Daisy is the most beautiful baby she's ever seen, and she's sorry that they live so far away.

I am getting further and further away from what is going on at Christmas dinner. I am thinking about Jack and how he will soon be here. Once he is here, in this house, the dynamic will change. I will be watching Jack as he works the room. I will be thinking about Jack kissing me.

I am busy getting the dinner dishes done, so that when Jack arrives, I can sit with him. James is wrapping leftovers and getting the coffee and desserts ready. There's a knock on the kitchen door. It's Jack. He's back. He is wearing jeans and a pale blue button down shirt. He comes in all smiles. But I can see there is some tension in his face. I lead him to the dining room and everyone welcomes him. Everyone except Breck, who hardly acknowledges Jack. After some coffee and dessert, Jack and I go into the family room to be alone.

"What a day!" Jack says, in a low voice. "Holidays are hard."

"Yeah?" I ask. "Things have been all right here. We just have one person who is a bit of a grouch."

"Breck?" Jack says. He nods. "Yeah, what's up with him?" he says. "I thought it was just me."

I shake my head. "I don't know. He's wife is so nice. She knit me a really pretty sweater. Mom really likes her, too. And, she is really good with Daisy."

Jack nods. "Like I said, holidays are not easy. My dad was in a bad mood. He won't say what's up, but he lets everyone know he's not happy. My sister was acting very bratty. She's always acting bratty, but especially so on holidays. My mom is very tense because she can't drink anymore. She really feels it around the holidays. These were the days that she would just coast through the celebration with a martini in hand. I have to say, I can relate. Uncle Aiden is his usual disciplined self, and-"

"Uncle Aiden? Here in New York?" I ask.

"Yep. He says he's here on business, but I think I'm the business he means. All in all, it's not so bad. My grandmother is nice, but she doesn't talk much. I have some really cute little cousins at the house. They've got like a million toys spread out all over the floor. It's making my Mom crazy," Jack says with half a smile.

"Just how many people are at your house?" I ask.

"We had about 35 people for dinner, but only about ten of them are staying with us."

"That's a lot of Christmas company," I say.

Jack nods. "Too much. I like a party of two," Jack says.

Then I tell Jack about how Gramps insisted that Rosey sit at the table with us. Jack is cracking up.

"If it makes Gramps happy, why not?" Jack says. "I guess so," I say.

"By the way, you look so pretty. I didn't even get to wish you a Merry Christmas!" Jack says.

He leans over and kisses me. His breath is sweet from the cookies he has just eaten. He smells like cologne. This is something new.

"Merry Christmas. I hope you are ready, Lacey. I am back," Jack says.

I smile. Butterflies are fluttering around in my stomach. It's the best and worst feeling. "You smell good."

"I got some cologne from my mom. You like it?" he asks. "I do."

Jack looks into my eyes. "All I did was think about you today," he says. I blush.

"Well, I didn't have time to think about you, Jacko. I had to help Mom, and then I played with Daisy, and I walked Rosey. I almost forgot that I would be seeing you today."

Jack puts his hand over my mouth to stop me from going on. I am smiling underneath his hand. "Now I know that is not true, Lacey. I know you thought about me. At least once."

I laugh and shake my head no.

Jack stands and takes something out of his pocket. "I've got something for you," he says.

"Jack? I didn't really get you anything good, just a stupid little coffee thing. I didn't want to jinx this, jinx us."

Jack puts his lips on mine. He kisses me for a long time. His kiss is so tender. Then he drops a black satin pouch in my hand.

"What's this?"

He shrugs his shoulders. I open the pouch and inside there is a necklace. Not just any necklace. It's a silver chain with a wishbone set in tiny diamonds. It's the most beautiful thing I've ever seen.

"Jack, what have you done?" I ask. "I can't accept diamonds from you."

Why not?"

I just look at him.

"Listen, I made a ton of money in California. This is nothing."

"This is so sublime! It's so pretty."

"It's a wishbone. I want you to make wishes on it. I hope your wishes come true." Jack is so romantic.

"I love the old necklace, Lace. But let's put this one on," he says. "Something about you and diamonds that gets me going," he says.

I nod. "Yes, but Jack, I love my silver heart necklace very much."

Jack takes off the silver necklace with the heart. "It's very pretty. But I like this one a whole lot more," he says. Then he puts on the diamond wishbone necklace. "I had this made for you. It's an original. Just like you, my love!"

"How does it look?" I ask. "Sparkling. Like you."

"I love it. I love it so much." I say.

"It was so hard to leave you. I kept thinking, I have to do whatever it takes to get back to her," Jack says.

"I'm so glad you're here, Jack. I didn't know that you would come back." There is silence and then Jack goes and does it.

"I love you!" he says.

This is such an intense moment. Jack is so wonderful, but this is all too much. He leans in for another kiss, but this one isn't so gentle. This one is passionate and strong. I can feel this kiss everywhere in my body. I am lost in this kiss.

We are making out, but I start to hear voices coming closer, so I break from the kiss. I look at the entranceway of the room, and there standing and watching me kiss Jack is Breck. It's creepy.

"Hello?" I say. Breck nods.

I pull away from Jack. "Is there something I can get you?" I ask Breck. "Nope. Just looking."

"Would you like to join us, Breck?" says Jack, trying to recover from the hot and heavy moment. Breck comes into the room and sits across from us and stares at us.

Oh joy.

Jack tries everything to get this guy to talk, but he doesn't say much other than, yes and no. Why doesn't he just get the hell out of here so I can go back to kissing my Jack?

"Hey, Jack," I say, "would you mind if I went to show my mom the necklace? I also want to take a look at it in the mirror."

"Of course not, babe. Take your time. Breck and I are fine, aren't we?" Jack says. Breck barely nods.

Jack winks at me.

In my room, I look at the necklace in the mirror, and I can't believe how beautiful it is on my neck. I go into the kitchen where Mom is talking to Arlene at the table. James is rocking Daisy to sleep in the background.

"Mom, look what I got from Jack," I say quietly. Mom turns to see the necklace. Her mouth drops open. "Wow. That is gorgeous!" she says.

"Oh my! It's a wish bone thing-a-ma-jig. So lovely!" says Arlene. "Diamonds? Oh my!" Mom doesn't know what to say or think.

James comes over to take a look.

"Wow!" he says. "I wish I could have gotten that for your mom," he says. "James, I loved your gifts," she says.

"Yes, but I didn't get you anything romantic. No diamonds, that's for sure," he says.

"Everything about you is romantic," she says. "Even your toes. Don't give it another thought." He laughs.

"Did he tell you to make a wish?" Arlene asks me. "Yes. Yes he did. And I'm going to," I say.

My wish is that Jack and I stay together forever. "Wear it in good health, dear," Arlene says to me.

I've never had something so extravagant. What does it mean if I accept this? Am I really Jack's girl? Are we back together for good? I need to take some time to think about this.

I text Becky to tell her that Jack has given me a diamond wishbone necklace. She writes back that Hoff has given her a fuzzy blanket and a pair of gloves.

I text back Merry Christmas.

Fifteen minutes later when I make it back to the family room, Gramps is now sitting almost on top of Jack, and is snoring away. Rosey is sleeping soundly next to Gramps.. And Breck is like a motor mouth talking Jack's ear off. Really?

"It aint easy, I'll tell you that," says Breck. Jack is nodding in agreement.

"I had a few false starts. It took close to five years, before I knew that I could really live without the stuff. But I had no choice. I wasn't a very nice drunk."

"Is anyone a nice drunk?" Jack asks.

"Well there are some people who don't come too undone. They just open up a bit. Alcohol lets them relax and feel comfortable in their skin. But nothing bad happens, you know? These people don't find themselves in the bar at four in the morning, pounding their fists on the table waiting for last call," Breck says.

Who would have thought that Breck and Jack would have something in common?

"I know it's not going to be easy, but if I want to accomplish my goals, drinking has no place in my life," Jack says.

Breck nods. "That's good. You have to keep at it. Constantly. Everything is about achieving a goal and not letting a drink get in the way."

"Definitely," says Jack.

"I've got 22 years of sobriety under my belt. I'm proud of it. But not a day goes by where I don't think about drinking."

I feel uncomfortable. Maybe this should be a private conversation. I decide to sit on Jack's other side, and close my eyes for a while. He puts his arm around me. I lean into him and think about the day. I love Christmas. I love the way everything always comes together. I love the way the house smells. I fall asleep in about four seconds. Hours later, Jack wakes me because he is going home. I snuggle up to him and kiss him goodnight, as he moves me onto the futon in Daisy's room, where I sleep soundly until the next morning.

Chapter Five

Life with Jack

A few days later, we are at the airport saying goodbyes. Arlene and Mom are hugging and kissing like old friends. Breck gives a cold wave and walks to the gate. He doesn't even bother to wait for Arlene. James says that his father is cold and unemotional. Mom tells James that he more than makes up for his father's shortcomings.

Four big things happen over the next few days.

The first big thing is that Arlene transforms Mom into a hottie. Her hair is now rich brown with burgundy highlights. Mom loves it. Everyone loves it. James says she looks like some actress, but he can't put his finger on the name.

The second big thing that happens is Beck takes me to her doctor and I am now officially on the Pill. I haven't told Jack this bit of news, because he's been checking out colleges in New York City and Boston. But he will be back in time for New Year's Eve. We have dinner plans at Blue, followed by an evening with Daisy. Mom and James are going to a party up the street, while we babysit for a few hours.

The next big thing that happens is Daisy gets a cold, and Mom and James freak out. In a panic, they rush to the doctor, only to learn that there is no cure for the common cold. People can travel to the moon, but they can't cure the common cold. Daisy just has to sweat it out. She's irritable, but after three days, she seems to be turning a corner. Unfortunately, Daisy manages to pass her cold on to her mother. Poor Mom is sniffling and sneezing.

The final big thing that happens is huge, even though I try to pretend that it is not big at all. I win a community journalism award. The prize is $2,500 toward college. Also, there is a dinner for me and my family to attend. I will be expected to accept the award and make a two-minute speech. I don't like speaking in front of people.

Mom is the one who opens the letter. Even though it is addressed to me, I hand it over to Mom. As she reads the letter, I can see happy tears streaming down her eyes. She jumps up and down and screams my name.

"You won the Terry Bradley Award!" she says.

"Oh yeah? What's that?" I ask, still not convinced that this is something to get excited about. "The English department at your school works closely with *The Daily Run*. They read your materials and select one student who shows the most promise in the field of journalism. You will be receiving $2,500 toward college, and you will have the opportunity to write a story for *The Daily Run*. In addition, you and your family will be invited to an awards dinner at The Grayson Mansion, where you will be expected to make a short acceptance speech. You will also have the opportunity to share some of your work," Mom says. "I'm so proud of you!"

"The Terry Bradley Award? I never heard of it," I say. "Who is Terry Bradley?"

"According to this letter, she was a writer and a teacher. When she died, she left a lot of money for a scholarship to be set in place for young writers," Mom explains.

I nod.

Something tells me that Ms. Gregory is behind this. That eager beaver guidance counselor!

"Lacey Ann Bryce, reporter at large!" says James. He is beaming, and really, it looks like he could not be any happier for me, and for Mom.

"Let's not get excited yet," I say. "Nobody said we were attending this thing," I say. How can I get out of this?

"You are not getting out of this," Mom shouts, and then she sneezes three times. She reaches for a box of tissues and blows her nose hard.

"Don't do that, Kate. You'll hurt yourself if you blow your nose too hard," says James.

He is very sweet with Mom.

Mom is not used to someone taking care of her. "Thank you, James," she says. "I'll be all right." James smiles at her.

"Wait 'til Gramps finds out," Mom says. "Wait 'til my mom hears about this."

"Kate, when is the awards dinner?"

"March 23rd," Mom answers.

"I'll bet my parents will want to come in for it," James says. "What? All the way from Ohio just for this stupid thing?" I say. "Absolutely," says James. He has a crazy smile on his face. "And Jack will definitely want to come!" Mom is beside herself.

Jack will want to come. Jack watching me make a speech about writing. How totally frightening.

The phone rings. That is something that almost never happens, and who is it? It's Ms. Gregory, calling to congratulate me. She wants me to know that this is me thinking about my future. Blah, blah, blah.

I hate the spotlight. I feel like I am under a microscope and all my flaws are bound to show when people are looking at me so closely.

But I have no choice but to go with this one. Luckily, I have more than three months to prepare for this event. Maybe I can convince everyone that it's really not important that we attend.

Later on in the day, Mason calls me to say that he heard that I am the recipient of the Terry Bradley Award. He, apparently, was hoping to win this award. He said he received a call that he came in third place in the creative writing category. Close, but no cigar.

Mason wants to go for coffee. Since Jack is not due back until the day after tomorrow, I agree. I am reluctant to go, because I never did tell Jack that I became friends with Mason after he went away. I don't think it will be a big deal to Jack, but I do feel like I should have told him.

I meet Mason at Starbucks and he has flowers for me, which is really sweet, but confusing. We sit down with our drinks, and a muffin to share.

"You are a rock star," Mason says. 'I hope you like carnations. They are all I can afford after Christmas."

I actually hate carnations.

"You shouldn't have, Mase. But it was sweet. Really sweet."

Mason has his board with him. He has a driver's license and he is planning on going to college in New England next year, but with the skate board, he just looks like a middle schooler. Like he should be wearing a name tag so that the bus monitors will know which bus he needs to get on.

I want to change the subject and ask about his Christmas, but Mason has his own agenda. He wants to talk about two things: Jack and the Terry Bradley Award. Those are two things that I don't feel like talking about.

"What did Jack say about the award?"

I shake my head. "He doesn't know yet. He's away visiting colleges."

"Oh yeah? Which colleges? Where does he think he's going?" Mason asks, trying to act like he's not that interested.

I shrug my shoulders. "Who knows?" I say.

"Is that why you are seeing me now?" Mason gives me a sneer. "Are you serious?" I ask.

"Well, I can't believe that Jack is so happy with us being friends. He was always a little jealous of me."

What? I don't say anything. I just gulp down my decaf latte. "He doesn't mind," I lie. "He trusts my ass."

"Really?" asks Mason.

"Shut up or I'll pour my coffee on your head."

"Ouch!"

Mason relaxes. He settles into his chair and breaks off a piece of the muffin. He is studying me. Why can't he like someone else?

"I just hope that you realize that this award is a really big deal. It's going to help you get into a really good college. You deserve it, Lace" he says.

"Thanks, Mason."

"I feel like we aren't friends anymore," he says. "We are friends," I say. I am uncomfortable. "Prove it."

"What the hell?" I say.

I want to get out of here. Starbucks is too loud and crowded today. And, every time I see Mason now, he hounds me about Jack.

"Tell me what you are writing about now," I ask, eager to change the subject. "Actually, I am writing about you." says Mason.

"Really now?" I ask. "That's a little creepy." I don't need anyone writing about me unless it's Jack.

"A love story. The girl is loosely based on you," Mason explains.

"You can't do that," I say.

"Why not? It's a free country," Mason says. "But it's not fair," I say.

"Loosely based," Mason repeats.

"That makes me uncomfortable," I say.

"Too bad. I can write about anything I want to write about. That's the joy of writing. I can write my own happy ending," Mason says, with a smirk.

"Let's get out of here and take a walk. I'll watch you do tricks on your skateboard," I say. Mason loves that. He is such a big showoff and he knows it.

If only I can get Mason to just relax about Jack, relax about us. Why can't he like someone else? Is it because he has a desire to have what Jack has? When is the last time that Mason hung out with Jack? I want to know this, but I don't want to give Mason the satisfaction of my curiosity.

We are at the park. I am holding the flowers Mason gave me. Mason cuts his wheels sharply and jumps. He turns and twists. He never loses his balance. I act like I'm all impressed for a while, but then I get tired of pretending to act like Mason is all that. He's just a little boy. I'm tired of his stupid little skateboarding show. I liked Mason when I first met him. He helped me through a difficult time. He got me writing. Not just thinking about writing, but actually writing. He's the only person who ever did that for me. But now, he's just obnoxious I stay a little while longer, and then I tell Mason I've got things to do. Before I step inside my house, I throw Mason's flowers away.

I have a decision to make. Do I tell my mom about the Pill or not? On the yes side, she will be relieved and I won't have to worry about her coming at me with questions about whether or not I'm having sex with Jack. On the no side, I don't want to talk about this stuff with Mom. It's uncomfortable. I decide to flip a coin. Heads, I will tell her. Tails, I will wait on it. And the winner is tails. That was easy.

On New Year's Eve day, Jack returns from looking at schools. He is picking me up at seven. I am wearing a royal blue mini dress and Mom's knee high, high-heeled black boots.

"Wow, you look so good," Mom says, coming into my room with Daisy in her arms. She sits on my bed and looks up at me.

Mom looks troubled. "What's wrong?" I ask.

Mom puts sleeping Daisy on my pillow and we both take a minute to stare at her. In the one month since she's been here, Daisy has grown a lot. She's still tiny, but her face has changed, her hands have gotten bigger, her fingers longer, and her tummy has filled out.

"I have to ask you something."

"All right."

"Are you and Jack having sex again?" she asks.

"Just get right in there and get to the point." I say. Mom giggles.

"I'm just trying to be proactive." Mom takes my hand.

"I know it's hard, and it's awkward. I just want you safe."

"I just got the Pill. I went with Becky." Mom looks sad.

"Don't be mad. You had a million other things to do. I haven't had sex with him again since you know what. He still doesn't know about the you-know-what. And I *will* tell him about the you- know-what. Soon. OK?"

Mom looks at me.

"Where did my little girl go?" she asks.

"Don't start that, Mom, or I will have to hit you." We both smile.

"I'm still getting used to you, Mom. Remember, a little over a year ago, you were a totally different person," I say.

A year ago I couldn't stand to be in the same room as Mom. So much has happened. And now. I love her to pieces, and not only do I love her, I like her.

"I know. It's new to me, too. Sometimes, I look at myself in the mirror and I don't know who the smiling woman is. I mean, I like who I am, it's just she's new. I don't know her that well."

"Well, she's got great hair," I say. I touch Mom's hair and play with it. Mom smiles because she loves her new look.

James comes in. "I got it. The name of the actress that you look like with your hair like that."

"Huh?" asks Mom.

"Julianne Moore. You are her double," James says. Mom and I laugh hysterically.

Jack looks so good. He is wearing boat shoes, khakis, and a light pink and white striped button down. He looks like an Abercrombie model. My Abercrombie model.

"Happy New Year, Lace. And let this be the start of an awesome year," Jack says. I smile and kiss him lightly on the cheek.

"So what's the plan," Jack asks me with Mom in the background.

"We are going to dinner and we will be back at nine. Then we will babysit while Mom and James go to the party."

"Listen, Jack, if you don't want to do that, we don't have to go to the party. I'm just as happy sitting home and staring at this little bundle of joy," Mom says.

"Don't be silly, Kate. We are excited about spending quality time with Daisy."

Dinner is so perfect. We are at the same place we had dinner the night we first slept together. Just being at this place is bringing back a flood of memories. So much has changed since we last came here. Jack has no idea of all these changes. And the fact that it is New Year's Eve is really making things feel strange. There are party decorations all over the place. People are dressed up, but still mellow, because it's early in the night. The waiters are walking around saying 'Happy New Year' every three seconds. We have a window table with a view of the water. Even at night, when it's totally dark, the view is beautiful.

Jack seems a little stiff in the restaurant. It was my intention to tell him that I have made friends with Mason. I wanted to bring it up casually. Say something like, "You know after you left, I started to hang out with Mason Cleets at Starbucks. Turns out, he is a writer, too. We're just friends." But I don't say this. I don't bring up Mason at all. Instead, I tell him about the writing award and he is overjoyed. "Are you kidding, Lacey? That is huge!" he says.

He leans over and kisses me. He rests his hand over mine.

I look out the window and I can see my reflection in the glass. I see my diamond wishbone glistening around my neck.

Jack is going on about how he is looking forward to the awards dinner. He picks up his glass of sparkling water and toasts me. I smile. I guess I am more excited about this than I have let on.

"I don't feel comfortable being in the spotlight," I say, quietly.

"It's not easy, but when you excel at something, you have to allow yourself to take the moment and be in it."

I nod. Jack is right.

"I can't wait to see you on the stage. I will be cheering for you." Jack reaches over and kisses me again.

"That's so great, Lace. Your mom must be tripping." I nod.

"She's tripping."

We sit at the table and look at each other for a moment.

"You know, I had two other girlfriends before you," Jack says. Oh. Where is this tidbit of information coming from?

"Two girls from church. Not at the same time," Jack chuckles. I roll my eyes.

"They couldn't hold a candle to you. They were girls. You are a woman." I blush.

"There's something about you. I don't know what it is," Jack says. I feel really, really, really uncomfortable.

"Is it my hair? My perky attitude? My push-up bra?" I try to joke.

"No. Those things are good, but it's something beyond all that. I don't know," Jack says. I am having trouble breathing.

The waiter comes and smiles at us.

"Do you folks know what you want?" he asks.

Oh, I think I know what I want. I'll have the Jack risotto. The Jack scampi. The Jack smothered in a lemon sauce. The Jack special. Why is this so much fun for me to think of dishes with Jack in them?

I order the broiled shrimp with rice and Jack gets a baked chicken dish with asparagus and sliced potatoes.

"I've got some news, too," Jack says. OK. Hit me with it.

"I'm going to college in the city. New York City," he says with a smile.

"Where?" I ask.

"Not sure where yet. I'll be just a stone's throw away from you. I'll see you on weekends. How does that sound?" Jack asks.

The truth is that sounds perfect. This is the best news. This means that I am in Jack's future. Not just his now, but his future. When he goes off to school next year, it won't mean goodbye. It will be different, but it will mean that Jack and I are together.

"I'm so happy!" I smile.

"I thought you might be," he whispers.

Our salads arrive. Jack has the Caesar. I have the mixed field greens with baby carrots and goat cheese.

"Do you want to taste my mixed field greens?" I ask Jack.

I stab some greens with my fork and hold it out to Jack, who opens his mouth.

"Oh that's good." Jack chews slowly with his mouth closed. "I don't know what's better, your salad, or having you feed me!"

Jack!" I laugh.

"I'm just being silly, Lace," he says.

"There's one thing I want to tell you, Jack," I say. "What's that, Lace?" he asks.

I feel shy and nervous all of a sudden. I think I might chicken out. I can't though. I've got to just say it. Say it. Say it. Say it.

"I'm on the Pill," I whisper. Jack looks at me with surprise. "Are you now?" he asks.

"Yep. We have to use condoms for a few more weeks until we are fully covered."

“You’ve been thinking about us hooking up, huh?” Jack asks.

“Yep,” I say.

“So in a few weeks no more condoms?” he asks. “You got it,” I say.

“It really *is* Christmas!” Jack says. I laugh.

“Who knows about this?” Jack asks, biting into a piece of bread. “Mom and Becky,” I say.

He nods.

“That’s good,” he says. “Really good.”

I am painfully aware that I have not broken my silence yet. I have not said anything about Mason, or more importantly, that after Jack left last summer, I found out that I was pregnant. I don’t say any of that, because it’s just too much to bear. I am a coward.

When we get home, Mom and James are dressed in party clothes. Mom is in black slacks and a cream colored satin halter. James is wearing black pants and a plaid button down shirt. Daisy is awake. She has just been changed and fed.

“How was it?” Mom asks.

“Excellent,” I say. “Jack, wasn’t it great?”

“It was,” says Jack. “I’m stuffed.”

After Mom and James leave, I rock Daisy to sleep, and transfer her to the crib. “That was relatively easy,” I say.

Jack is smiling at me. I am so eager to touch him, I could scream. But, of course, that would wake Daisy, and I definitely don’t want to wake up Daisy.

We go into the family room, so that we are close enough to hear Daisy, in case she wakes up. “Let’s party,” says Jack.

I'm confused for a minute. I picture Jack taking out his flask or smoking a joint. That was what he meant in the past when it was time to party. Now it means something different.

"You're my party," Jack says.

I am standing a few feet away from him. I have a serious expression on my face. My heart is racing.

"Come here," Jack says. "No," I say. "You come here."

Jack just looks at me. The smile is gone from his face. It's like we are playing a game. It's very exciting.

Jack looks determined. Hungry. He takes me in his arms and I am gone. I can feel myself floating on a cloud. A Jack cloud.

My dress comes off. Then my bra and my tights are off. Jack's clothes are off. He lifts me on the couch. He pauses to put on the condom. I make sure that it is on correctly. From what I can tell, that sucker is completely covering Jack. Soon, he is inside me. My face is in the contours of his neck. I cry out briefly. He looks into my eyes. Never closes them. Wants to watch me the whole time. After, I cannot move.

"Happy New Year!" he says.

"Right back at you."

There is more kissing and touching. I want him again just minutes after I had him. He wants me too. We end up on the floor with me on top. He takes my breath away. I am left struggling to catch my breath. Jack is smiling. Never takes his eyes off me. This is so hot.

Being naked with Jack, I feel pure. Maybe that is the opposite of what I should feel, but my mind doesn't work that way. I feel natural. Jack is a puzzle piece and I am a puzzle piece and we fit together. Like peas in a pod. Like ice cream in a cone. Like ink in a pen. We belong together.

"Jack, when I'm with you, I'm different," I say. "Different how?" he asks.

"I don't know. I just want to touch you and be with you. Is that wrong, Jack? Is it wrong to want to be on top of you and all over you? Sometimes, I feel dirty."

Jack studies me for a while.

"It's not wrong. It feels right," Jack says. "It feels like it's the only thing to do. That's not dirty, Lace. It's awesome."

We kiss because that is the only thing to do and it feels right.

Later, we are dressed and eating milk and cookies on the floor. Jack and I are talking about the highlights of the year. I know this is a perfect opportunity to tell him about the low points of the year: the day he left me, the moment I realized I was pregnant, the second they told me that I had a miscarriage. I know I should tell him. I look at him, and he is just waiting to hear what I have to say. But that's when Daisy starts to scream. She must be having a nightmare.

Jack takes her out of the crib and starts to dance around the room with her. He dims the lights and plays soft music. Daisy likes this. Then I heat up a bottle and Jack feeds it to her. We sit together on the couch, watching Daisy.

"Two minutes until midnight," Jack says.

It's an exciting and romantic countdown. At the stroke of midnight, Jack kisses me softly and deeply and it's all I ever wanted.

Chapter Six

Getting Settled

I am so busy these days. I barely have time for Becky. I am either doing schoolwork, writing for the local paper, which I get paid for, hanging out with Jack, or watching Daisy for Mom.

Otherwise, I am sleeping. Jack is busy, too. Unfortunately, he had to give up football because of everything going on in his life, but he is psyched about being able to play lacrosse in the upcoming weeks. I am excited to see him play. I never had a boyfriend who played sports.

Actually, I never had a real boyfriend.

I will have to make time to get to some of his games. Mom is going back to work in a few weeks and she has been really crabby about it. James wants her to extend her maternity leave, but she says that we really can't afford to do that right now. She says we need the money coming in.

They have been interviewing babysitters almost every day for the last couple of weeks. Mom hasn't found anyone that she likes.

Today, Jack and I have plans to take Gramps to lunch. We've never done this before, and I am excited about it. As we head to his house, Jack is playing Jack Johnson songs and singing to me.

"I love you, Jack, but you are a terrible singer," I say.

He just laughs.

"And, I don't like Jack Johnson."

"How could you not like Jack Johnson?" Jack asks. "He's boring. I'd much rather listen to the Stones."

"You need some variety," Jack says. "I don't need variety," I say to Jack. He winks at me.

I have a special doggy treat for Rosey-O. I can't wait to give it to her. Ever since Rosey came into Gramps' life, Gramps has been so much more pleasant.

Jack parks his car in the driveway, and we head to the front of the house. I have a few things for Gramps, including some fresh black and white cookies, which he says he loves. We used to split them in half. Vanilla for me, chocolate for Gramps.

It's odd for the front door to be closed. Usually, when Gramps is expecting company, he has the front door ajar. Immediately, I am concerned.

"Wonder why the door isn't open," I say.

"Well, let's find out," Jack says. He kisses the top of my head. "Gramps? Hey, you dressed?" I call out.

The door is shut, but it's not locked.

Rosey is barking up a storm. She runs toward us and it's not her usual bark. Something is very wrong.

"Where is he?" I ask. 'Something's up."

I look around the place. It's filthy. It smells really bad. I have to put my hand over my nose, or I might gag. Gramps is not on the couch. He's not in his room. He's not in the bathroom.

Jack goes into the kitchen and calls out my name. "Lacey. He's in here."

Gramps is in the kitchen, all right. He's on the kitchen floor and he's unconscious. Jack takes out his phone and calls 911.

I become hysterical.

"He's breathing, but he's unconscious. I think he may have slipped," Jack says, and points to the spill on the kitchen floor.

"I need help, please. My girlfriend's grandfather is unconscious. We just got here, and I'm not sure what happened. He has a pulse. Yes. 36 Mockingway Terrace, Island Park. That's right.

Yes. Hurry," Jack says.

"Oh my God! Gramps!" I cry.

"I don't know what to do. Jack, should I call my mother, or should I wait until the ambulance comes? I don't know what to do. Poor Rosey. She's so scared. It's all right, baby." I take Rosey in my arms.

But Jack is in control. He is already dialing my mother. Perfect Jack. He is speaking very calmly and giving her the details. Telling her to try to relax. I can hear her cry out in the background.

Jack reassures her by telling her that Gramps has a pulse. Jack promises to call her as soon as the paramedics leave. In the meantime, she is on the way.

By the time help comes, I am sobbing. What happens if he dies? What am I supposed to do? I know he's old, but he's not that old. I just need him in my life now. It would be so unfair if this was it for him. Mom would not be able to deal with that.

Jack pulls me away from Gramps so that the two men, who have arrived in emergency medical outfits can do their job. The men work quickly and quietly. They put Gramps on a stretcher and wheel him out to the ambulance. I take Rosey in my arms.

We are on our way to Roosevelt Hospital. Again. I know the place well. Irony. It's where I had my, um, where I was pregnant. It's where Mom delivered Daisy.

Jack and I follow the ambulance. I am crying and Rosey is shaking, but Jack is strong. He puts his hand over mine, and tells me that he has a feeling that Gramps is going to be all right.

I call Mom from the road. She is crazy with fear. James is at a kids' sporting event, but he is meeting us in the parking lot as soon as he can break away. Jack will sit in the car with Rosey and Daisy until we find out what we are dealing with.

We are in the parking lot waiting for my mom. Jack tells me if I want to go into the hospital, I can, and then my Mom will just meet me in there. I am afraid to do that. If it's something really bad, I don't want to have to face it alone. Jack puts his arms around me and Rosey.

"I see Mom's car. She sees us," I say. I wave to her.

Mom manages to park a few spots away from Jack's car. Daisy is sleeping in her car seat.

Jack will sit in Mom's car and watch Daisy and Rosey. When I know what's going on, I'll come out to give Jack a report.

Mom takes my hand and we walk toward the emergency entrance. "What happened?" she asks.

"We got there and the door was shut, and I said, I wonder why the door is shut. That's not like Gramps when he knows someone is coming over. Jack found him on the floor in the kitchen. Jack thinks he might have fallen. I don't know."

Mom squeezes my hand as we enter the hospital, and I start asking questions about where we can find Gramps. We are told to wait in the waiting room. There is a doctor examining him now.

Waiting. It's so hard. Not knowing.

"I'm Dr. Gladston, and you must be Kate," says a good-looking doctor with a crooked smile. "How's my father doing?" Mom asks.

"He's all right. I think he was dizzy when he slipped. We are running some tests, but he seems all right, for the most part. He told me that he lives alone."

Mom nods. "I live about twenty minutes away," Mom explains. "I try to check in on him at least once a week."

"Sure. I think you might want to think about making other plans for him. Living alone might be more than he can handle now," says Dr. Gladston with his crooked smile.

Mom and I were not expecting to hear that. Poor Gramps.

"You can go see him now. I think we will keep him overnight, just to make sure he doesn't have a concussion," Gladston says.

When I come into the room, Gramps is looking at me funny. "Gramps!" I say.

He is definitely confused and I feel so bad. It must be awful not to be sure of the people in your life. I take his hand. "I love you. Gramps," I say.

Sometimes, it's as if he doesn't hear me. But I don't give up.

"Don't worry about Rosey-O. She is in good hands. Jack is watching her in the parking lot." Again, Gramps has a confused look.

"You are going to be fine, Gramps."

"It's all right," says Mom. "Dad, how are you feeling?" she asks.

"Kate? Is that you, Kate? Come in and say hello to your dad. What did you bring me? Any cookies?"

Gramps takes Mom's hand and looks at her.

"What a day!" he says. "I fell. Did you hear?" he asks.

Mom nods. "I heard. Pop, what are we going to do with you?"

Gramps has to stay in the hospital for two days while they run some tests. In that time, Mom spends a lot of time talking to James with the door closed. I am not sure what's going on. After a while, Mom comes to me and tells me that she has made a decision.

Mom is going to extend her maternity leave through the school year. That means she won't be earning her salary. She will not go back to teaching until the next school year. Gramps will move into our house. Mom is going to take care of Daisy and Gramps. It won't be easy, but Mom feels that this is the best decision for everyone.

When Mom breaks the news to Gramps, he is less than thrilled.

"I can't live with you," he says. "You're too demanding!" Gramps says.

Mom's eyes bulge out of their sockets. "I'm demanding? You are a pain in the ass!"

"I won't do it, Kate," he says.

But when Mom explains that it is either our house, or a nursing home, Gramps no longer objects. Cleaning out his house and selling it is not easy and most of the work falls on James. Gramps is left with a suitcase filled with junk. Everything else has been tossed or sold. Gramps has one photo album that he holds close to his heart. He says this is where all his memories are.

I think to myself, if I had to put everything that was special to me in one suitcase, how would I choose? What would I keep? What would I toss? I know I would keep Libby. She's the only thing I have from my dad. I would keep the poem that Jack wrote to me asking me to his semi-formal. I would keep the two necklaces I got from him. I would keep my journals. It would be hard to toss all the other stuff. I've always thought a person is equal to the sum of his or her belongings. But maybe that's not true. Maybe who you are has nothing to do with what you own.

Chapter Seven

Changing Focus

It was an adjustment when James moved into the house. It was one more person to share two tiny bathrooms. I had to get used to always being dressed, setting the table for three, and always getting him and Mom together, never just Mom. If I had a question for mom, chances are James was going to give an answer, too. I had to get used to being the third wheel. Mom and James are the couple, and I was the outsider. Then there was an adjustment when Daisy came. There was getting used to all the crying and the crazy hours she kept. I had to get accustomed to having Mom on her terms. If she was talking to me, she was also nursing Daisy, or rocking her, or dressing her. Daisy took up everyone's time and since she was the smallest person in the house, she required the most care. And now there is another adjustment: getting used to Gramps living in the house. The first thing I lose is my bedroom. I say that I don't mind and that I would do anything for Gramps, but the fact still remains, I lost my bedroom, and the only stitch of privacy that I had. I have my choice. I can sleep on the futon in Daisy's room, or on the couch in the new family room. Either way, there is no privacy. I am out in the open. All my stuff is still in my room, but now I am roomless. And, also there is the adjustment of Rosey-O. I love her to pieces, but when did I sign on to walk her and feed her? Having a dog is like a full-time job and somehow, it became my job. Gramps just expects me to take care of her. He never even says thank you.

James talks about turning the porch into a bedroom for me, but it just sounds too complicated. I feel like I sound selfish. They have enough to deal with, and if James has to start building walls, and painting, Mom won't be able to rely on him for help with the baby or Gramps. So I just accept the fact that I am on the couch. I've got my journals and my jewelry box and my books in a few shoeboxes on the floor of my closet. I have my pink blankey and my pink bathrobe, and

it's all good. Mom is the one who is really losing her mind. Gramps is always criticizing her. And he never says please or thank you.

If Mom makes Gramps a roast beef sandwich for lunch, he might say: "Why did you make me a roast beef sandwich, Kate? You know I like turkey. Don't you listen?"

So, the next day, Mom will make Gramps a turkey sandwich.

"Turkey? I don't like turkey, Kate. You know that," he might say.

She can't win. The doctor told her that she can't take any of it personally. So Mom tries not to argue with Gramps. She has this thing now, where she closes her eyes and counts to ten. She says it helps her deal with him. By the time she is on nine or ten, she doesn't care that much. If you ask me, Mom is a time bomb. She is definitely going to lose it one day with Gramps. I just hope I am at school or out with Jack when it happens.

Mom loves being home with Daisy. A lot of times, I find them on the floor in the nursery. Mom will be reading books to Daisy in those playful voices of hers. Daisy will be cooing with her feet in the air. Every once in a while, Mom will laugh out loud in response to Daisy's expression.

When that happens, Mom knows that she did the right thing by staying home with Daisy. But then there are the moments when Daisy won't stop crying, Gramps is grumpy, and Mom hasn't even had a chance to brush her hair.

I have to come home right after school just to walk Rosey. Whenever I forget, Mom gives me a major attitude. She goes on about how I need to take responsibility. I get really mad when she goes on like that. I didn't ask to take on the dog. I try to spend some quality time with Gramps every day. I ask him about his day. He always has something negative to say about the lunch Mom made him. I try to ignore that. Then I might go out for an hour or two to see Jack. I'm usually home in time to help make dinner. Sometimes Jack comes over and helps, and we all eat dinner together. Sometimes, Jack and I bring sandwiches from his family deli for dinner, just to make thing easier on Mom. She really appreciates that. James isn't home as much as when the baby was first born. He is coaching sports, in order to make more money. When he gets home, the first thing he does is kiss Mom. It's kind of gross, but it's nice. Then he goes to Daisy and holds her up in the air. She squeals in delight. He makes funny faces for her and she laughs.

Then James makes small talk with Gramps. James is always trying to give Mom a little time to herself. He tells her to go get her nails done, go meet a friend, or take a long, hot shower. Most of the time, Mom just takes a nap. It looks like having a baby is totally exhausting. Sometimes, I have to get away from the people in my house. That's when I go to Jack's.

I have dinner with Jack and his family a few times.

Julie, Jack's mother is not as nice as she was when I first met her. She is the nervous type. At the dinner table, she constantly bites her nails. She doesn't eat much, which is funny since she runs a catering business. She just pushes her food back and forth on her plate. She reminds me of a bird. She is always looking at Jack and thinking something. I think she must be overprotective and overly involved. I try not to notice, but it does make me a little uncomfortable.

Julie doesn't like the fact that Jack and I are so close. She hates that he puts his arm around me at the table, or plays with my hair while we are sitting in the living room. She hates that Jack is his easygoing self with me.

Jack doesn't get too involved with his mother's behavior. When we are at the table with his family, Jack practically gives me all his attention.

"So, Lacey, Jack tells me that you are getting a journalism award," she says. I blush. Thanks, Jack.

"Yes," I say.

"Well, dear, that's very special. Are you planning on going to school for writing?" she asks, as she tucks her short blond hair behind her ears.

I nod.

"I think so. Maybe. I don't know," I say, sounding like a moron.

"You bet she's going to school for writing. She's going to be a reporter for *The New York Times*!" Jack says, winking at me.

"I am?" I ask.

"Well, you have so much more time to decide. Jack will be going off to school before we know it, but you will have another year of high school," Julie says.

What a bitch. This is her way of saying that whatever we have doesn't really matter because Jack is going off to school this year, and I'm not.

I smile politely.

"That's all right. Lacey is so much more mature than me. It will give me a chance to catch up to her," Jack says.

Julie ignores Jack's comment. "It's wonderful to be able to write well," Julie says. "I wish you could give Adrian some tips on writing."

Adrian rolls her eyes and stabs her steak with her fork.

Adrian is a brat. I also think there may be something wrong with her. She is always pouting and she doesn't make eye contact with people when they speak to her. Her behavior does not fit her age. She acts five, but she is really ten. But I smile at her and try to make peace at the table.

"Don't be such a spoiled brat," Jack says to her.

"I am not being a spoiled brat. I just don't have anything to say about writing, OK?" she says.

"That's all right!" I say. "What do you like to do?" I ask, trying to make conversation. "Nothing, I don't like anything," she says, giving me a nasty glare.

"Do you like playing with your computer?" I ask, because every time I see her, she has her iPad in her hand.

"Maybe," she says.

"Well, that's something. What do you like to do on it?" I ask. "I don't know," she says.

"Do you like games, or reading, or social media, or," Julie interrupts me.

"Adrian is not allowed on social media," says Julie.

"Really?" Jack asks. "She may not be allowed on it, but she is definitely on it."

"Adrian, you know you are not allowed on social media" Julie says.

"Everyone is on social media," Adrian says.

"You are not allowed, Adrian. You know that," says Julie. Her face is stern and her voice is threatening.

"That's not fair," Adrian cries out.

"It's true, Ma, everyone is on social media. Even Lacey's grandfather," says Jack, trying to soften the blow for his little sister.

"Adrian, we need to talk," Julie says.

Adrian looks at her mother with contempt. She doesn't say anything and for a second, I think she is going to throw her steak at her mother.

"Adrian, you are excused," Julie says.

Adrian pounds her fist on the table. She looks over at her dad for support.

"We can talk about this later," Dad says.

"I hate this family," Adrian says, as she makes her way out of the fancy dining room.

Julie looks at me and gives me a small smile.

"Well, I guess that's a good sign that we can all be our true selves around you, Lacey." What a stupid remark.

I nod. "By the way, the chicken is delicious," I say with a bright smile. So the family is definitely a bit dysfunctional.

But now that lacrosse season has begun, Jack's family goes to all his games. I try to go to at least one game a week. It's so cool to see Jack on the field. He's so fast and he scores a lot of points. Jack's mom, dad, and sister all act very differently when they are at the games. Julie smiles and chats with the other moms. She acts all happy and easygoing. Jack's dad keeps his arm around Julie and cheers on the team. Adrian occasionally smiles and roots for her brother. The family always donates a tray of sandwiches to the team after each game if they win. Whenever I come to the game, I drag Becky with me. I get a kick out of watching Jack, but I don't really like sitting with Jack's family. Becky calls them the Monsters.

Jack says he feels more comfortable with my family than he does when he is with his family. I like that because my family may be a little quirky, but they are certainly warmer than Jack's family. My mom has hugged Jack a few times, and James often jokes around with Jack. Julie has never so much as touched me, and Jack's father does not speak to me, unless Julie prompts it.

One interesting thing is that lately, Jack hardly ever goes with his family to church. I haven't said anything to him about it, but it's interesting that it doesn't seem as important as it used to be.

Jack decides to go to New York University (NYU) in the fall. It's only an hour train ride from my house. Not bad at all. When Jack takes me to see the campus, we walk around the Village. I have always loved that area of the city. We sit in Washington Square Park and watch the kids skateboarding. It's a cold day in late February, but the sun is shining and it feels good on our faces. While we sit on a bench, we see a guy cop some weed from another guy.

Jack is thinking about something.

"It's hard, Lace," Jack says in a soft voice.

I look at him in his blue down jacket. His eyes are like dark blue marbles. He's holding my hand and I purposely have my gloves off so that I can feel his skin next to mine.

"What's hard?" I ask.

"Giving it up. Giving it all up," he says.

"You mean drinking and weed?" I ask.

He nods. He looks away from my gaze.

"Sometimes, I think I can get away with just one more night of drinking. I still think about it. I just want to relax sometimes, and it's the only way I know how to really let go."

I don't know what to say. I'm so glad he can be honest with me, but I really don't know what to say to help him out.

"I haven't had any drinks or smoked weed since you came back to me on Christmas Eve. And this is the first time I am even thinking about it. I'm sorry it's hard for you, Jack. Really," I say.

"I think about it a lot. Sometimes more than other times. When things go well, it's easier. I can walk away and not feel like I'm missing something. But when something doesn't go my way, even if we lose a game, or my mom pisses me off, I just want to get high," he says.

"So what do you do," I nestle closer to him on the bench.

He reaches toward my face and kisses me lightly. I lean forward for a longer kiss, but he doesn't accept my offer.

"I go for a run, or I get busy with something, and that helps. Sometimes, I even call someone like Breck."

"Breck?" I ask. "James' dad?"

"Yes."

"What?" I ask.

"When I met him at Christmas, he gave me his number and told me to call him whenever I wanted to talk about stuff. He's a really good influence. He's a really smart guy."

"How come you didn't tell me?" I ask.

"I don't know. I didn't mean to keep it secret, it's just, I don't know," he says.

I don't know what to make of this. So whenever Jack feels like drinking, he gives old Breck a call. That just seems so strange.

"The guy *was* able to talk to you. He doesn't seem like he can talk to anybody else, though." I say.

"That's his personality and the fact that he's an alcoholic," Jack says.
"That's odd," I say.

"What?" asks Jack.

"I don't know. You talking to Breck. Does James know?" I ask.

"I don't know. Breck doesn't really talk to James," he says.

"I noticed that."

"Uncle Aiden says it's helpful to talk to people who are in the same boat. That's kind of the way AA works. You surround yourself with people who also can't drink. You share a common theme," he explains.

"Do you go to AA meetings?" I ask.

"I went to a few, but it wasn't my scene. I don't like the idea of talking to strangers."

"How does your mom stay sober?" I ask.

"Church helps her, but, really, she's a mess all the time."

"Does she go to meetings?" I ask.

"I don't think so. She keeps things quiet. You know, like if you don't talk about the problem, there is no problem. I don't like that. I think we all have to talk about what we're feeling, even if it sucks," Jack says.

"Yeah, I guess," I say.

"You don't sound convinced," Jack says.

"Sometimes, I think it's better to just leave things alone. Not drag them up and talk about them. Sometimes, the talking isn't going to solve anything. It's not going to change the facts," I say.

"Maybe. But I think we all have to be able to say what's on our minds. Work through any shit, you know?" he says.

"Gramps says that he and my grandmother never went to bed mad at each other. They talked through things, even if they had to get up early the next day. Gramps says it was the key to a good marriage," I say.

"Gramps is a very smart man," Jack says, and smiles at me.

We sit in silence for a while. I didn't know that Jack still thinks about partying. I want to talk more about this, but I also want to just run from this conversation.

We walk through the park and down West Fourth Street and we go in and out of some cute one- of-a-kind shops. Jack buys me a headband and a pair of fuzzy socks. Then we go to the NYU store and Jack and I get matching NYU sweatshirts. He's really going off to college. I'll be stuck in high school and he will be in the big city. But, we will have matching sweat shirts.

The subject of Jack's drinking doesn't come up again. "I'm going to see if I can live in a single room," Jack says. "Really?" I ask.

"That way when you come for weekends, we can be alone. It will be sublime," Jack smiles.

"Are you sure, Jack? I'm not sure that you should do that. It might be good for you to have roommates. Isn't that part of the fun of college?" I ask.

"Well, to be honest, it's not just because of my love and lust for you that I want a single. I think it would be easier for me to deal with things. Chances are, roommates will want to party and it will be easier if I am in a room by myself. That way, I can always go back to my room if things get out of hand."

"I see your point," I say.

"I don't know, we'll see. It's six months away. Maybe in six months, I won't be thinking about drinking."

Jack kisses my head and we continue to wander through the Village.

After Jack drops me home later that night, I find James in front of the TV in the living room. He's watching a basketball game. He's got a beer in one hand, and he's talking back to the TV about the players and the game. Mom and Daisy have gone to bed and Gramps is playing solitaire.

"Hey," I say.

"Hey, how was the big day at NYU?" James asks.

"Great. I love it there. Jack is psyched."

James laughs. "I'll bet. Great area." James puts the empty beer bottle on the table. "James, did you know that Jack sometimes calls Breck?" I ask.

James looks at me funny. "How would I know something like that? You know I don't really talk to Breck. What, they talk about being sober?" he asks.

"Yes. How did you know that?" I ask.

"Well, I know Breck has a good heart. If he can help a fellow drinker, he will. Over the years, he has helped a lot of young people. He makes himself available to them."

"That's a good thing, I think, right?" I ask.

"Yes, it's a good thing. I'm glad. Breck doesn't really have such good communication skills with the people in his family, so it's nice that he can reach out and help a person in need."

James means what he says. He seems all right with the fact that Jack and Breck are friends and we have nothing to do with that.

"Are your parents coming anytime soon?" I ask.

"As a matter of fact, Lace, they are," James says, and then he smiles big.

"Are they really coming in for the dumb awards dinner? Please say they are not."

"Of course they are. They are all excited about it. They are going to be staying in a hotel. This way, we won't be on top of one another. They will be here with us for about a week."

"Oh my God. They are coming all the way from Ohio for this dumb thing? How am I going to get through this night?" I ask.

"Get through it? No, Lacey, you aren't going to just get through it. You are going to shine. How's the speech coming along?"

I nod. It is so not coming along. I don't have a speech. I have nothing.

"Your mother has been looking forward to this since she read the acceptance letter," James says, laughing.

"A little pressure, huh?" I ask.

"Hey," says Gramps. "Pipe down!" His tone is especially nasty.

We turn and look at Gramps, who has his cards spread all over the coffee table. "I can't even hear myself think with the two of you yapping away."

James and I look at each other like we can't believe Gramps.

"The nerve!" I say, but I'm smiling because I know that even though Gramps is a grump, he loves having us around him.

"Good night, grumpy Gramps," I say, as I go into the family room with Rosey following me.

Chapter Eight

You're Unbelievable

On the day of the awards dinner, I am sick to my stomach. Throughout the school day, I experience major waves of nausea. Becky says it's just nerves, but I am convinced that I am dying of food poisoning.

Becky offers to straighten my hair, and listen to me do my speech after school.

"Here's what you do when you feel nervous. You pretend everyone in the audience is naked. That's what you do," Becky says.

We are sitting in the family room. Becky is straightening my hair. Daisy is in her play seat watching me, and doing raspberries.

Becky is drinking a huge glass of milk and eating chocolate chip cookies. "I can't even watch you eat that without feeling like I'm going to hurl."

"Have you spoken to Jack?" she asks.

I nod. "He texted me early this morning. Said he would meet me there tonight. Said he couldn't wait to see me accept the award. I want to vomit." I speak in a monotone voice. I don't know why I am speaking like this.

"The way you're talking is not going to work when you do your speech, Lace. Cut it out, or it's going to stick in your mind."

"You are right," I say, in the same monotone voice.

"By the way, what about Mason, skate-boarder dude? Is he going to be there tonight?" Becky asks.

"Probably. Ugh. That makes me uncomfortable. I never did tell Jack that Mason and I are friends. It's just that in the past few months, we really haven't hung out at all. It didn't seem like there would be a point to telling him," I say.

"He seems a little creepy," Becky says.

I nod in agreement.

"Did I tell you that Hoff and I are going to Florida for spring break?" I shake my head.

"Um, I think I would have remembered that detail," I say, in my monotone voice.

Becky smiles. Her whole face lights up as she is thinking about spring break with Hoff.

"We got cheap fares and we are staying one night in a hotel, and three nights at his aunt and uncle's house. It should be cool. Hoff and I are getting matching board shorts."

"That will be a sight. The two tallest people on the beach wearing matching outfits," I say.

Becky is concentrating now. She's done the back of my hair, and the sides, and now she has to get my side bangs just right. I don't interrupt her. I know this is the sort of thing that can make it or break it.

"Don't breathe," Becky says.

Of course, this is when Daisy starts to wail and go crazy. Sometimes, I think she knows when everyone is counting on her to be a quiet little baby. Those are the times, she often goes nuts. Her scream is so high-pitched, it's scary.

"Holy shit!" Becky says.

I smile. I am used to it by now. I give Daisy a silly face, and for a second she stops screaming. Mom comes in with Rosey-O practically attached to her leg.

"Did someone call?" she asks Daisy.

Daisy immediately stops crying and looks at Mom and smiles. Mom smiles back. James says that Daisy and Mom have totally bonded. I'd have to agree.

"Hey, Kate, want me to do your hair for you?" Becky asks, letting a soft burp fall out of her mouth.

"Oh, Beck, I'd love that," Mom says. "You always do such a nice job."

"How do I look?" I ask Mom and Becky and they both smile and nod their heads. "Gorgeous," says Mom. "A knock out. A star. My little girl," says Mom.

"Like you are ready for the runway. The literary runway," Becky jokes.

Mom and Becky hug me. Mom has tears in her eyes. "Tears of happiness," she says.

I like the hair. I like my black dress and the ballet pink cardigan. I like my black tights, and black heels. I like my diamond necklace. It's me I don't like. I hate my speech. It's bullshit. It's about what writing means to me and it doesn't make any sense.

"I'm not giving that speech, Becky," I say.

"What are you talking about? Of course you are, Lace. It's a great speech. Perfect, really," she says.

"No. It's a stupid speech from a fake girl. I'm not using that speech. I don't have a speech," I say, in that old monotone voice.

I am making Becky crazy. She is holding my wrists to try to get me to promise that I will just do the speech as is.

But I won't. I'd rather go up there and have nothing to say, than to say that garbage.

Gramps is dressed in brown dress pants and an orange plaid shirt. He is too cute for words. Mom is wearing a gray skirt, a pink sweater, and black heels. James is in a dark suit. His parents have arrived from Ohio, and are meeting us at the place. We have to leave in a few minutes. We are just waiting on the babysitter. The babysitter is late. Mom is not happy. I decide to take my own car so that I will have a few minutes to get prepared.

Becky hugs me and wishes me the best night.

I drive over to the place. I search for Jack's car, but I don't see it yet. In my haste, I realize I forgot my phone. Typical. I walk into the place and I am greeted by several people who are working the event. I introduce myself and explain that I am one of the people who will be getting an award tonight. Everyone is very nice. A photographer asks to take my photo. I am not pleased, but I can't really say no. I make a fake smile, and then turn my fake smile into a stern ugly face, and that's right when the photographer takes the shot. Excellent.

No Jack. But I see Arlene and Breck. Arlene is dressed in a teal blue pant suit that probably was stylish thirty years ago, and Breck is in a suit that he's probably been wearing for thirty years.

They see me and come toward me. Arlene is smiling and waving. Breck has a straight face on. "Hello," I say.

Arlene grabs hold of me and squeezes me. Breck gives me a slight smile. "Thank you so much for coming. Really, it was so nice of you."

"Don't be silly, dear. This is fun for us. Tell me, are they bringing the baby?"

"No," I say. "Daisy would not do well here. Whenever it needs to be quiet, she is loud. It's just the way it is."

Arlene laughs and Breck nods his head. "Is Jack here?" Breck asks.

"Not yet," I say.

Gradually, people start to come in and fill the room. We have our own table, and it is very close to the stage. That will make it easier, I think. I will be able to look at Jack while I do my speech, and things won't be that overwhelming.

Mom rushes toward me and squeezes my shoulder. She whispers in my ear that I look beautiful. I nod. I don't feel beautiful. Nerves make me feel ugly. James finds his parents and they rush to Mom. Mom and Arlene embrace. Breck gives Mom a kiss on the cheek, and tells her that she looks very well. Mom beams.

There are a few people from the school district that Mom and James know. I watch, as my mother, makes her official comeback to the school district. Her principal is there and she is talking to my mother with a big smile.

Mom is good at talking to people. Why am I terrible at it? Is this the genetics of my father being passed down? Probably. Why must I be a bundle of nerves? Where is Jack? This is not like him.

A man in a black suit with a full head of white hair comes up onto the stage. All the people in the room begin to quiet down. The man introduces himself. I can't remember his name. He talks briefly about how writing has become a lost art, and how we need to do whatever we can to strengthen the writing skills of our students. I lose him on the sixth or seventh sentence. I go to a place where panic lives. Is something wrong? Why hasn't Jack come?

I do not know where he can be. There is a lump in my throat the size of a shoe. I am not sure what could have happened. Did he have to work at the deli? In his text this morning, he said he would see me there. Here. I am painfully aware of the empty seat next to me. Mom is sitting on my other side. James is next to her. Breck is next to him. Arlene is next to him. Gramps is next to her. Where is Jack? I know Breck is wondering the same thing. I see him look through the crowd. I can tell he is looking for his buddy Jack. As I glance around the room, I am calculating how many people must be here. I am working my estimating skills, which Jack would be proud of. If every table has anywhere from six to eight people, and I count 25 tables that means there are about 175 people here, most of whom, are adults. I am one of six high schoolers to be receiving an award.

As I scan the room, I make an observation that leaves me unsettled. Mason Cleets is not here. I didn't think he would have missed this event. What could that mean? Did something happen at Jack's school today? Was there an emergency assembly tonight for seniors? Did something happen at the Tolland school? Was there a shooting? I don't understand. Of course, I know that this is partly my fault because I forgot my damn phone. There are probably messages and texts from Jack, explaining that he was delayed and that he will be here in five. Unless, maybe his mom or dad had a heart attack. That could have happened. Jack would explain that he is at the hospital, but he will definitely be sure to catch the tail end of my speech on the way home. Or, Adrian is in the hospital, because she stuck her finger in an electrical socket and she needs to have brain surgery to restore the damage.

I don't know where Jack is and it's killing me. Literally. With each second that goes by, I am losing my mind. I go deeper and deeper into a state of panic on the inside. On the outside, I am still pretending like everything is perfect. I have a small smiled pursed on my lips, and I gaze at Arlene as if I am smelling flowers. Mom has her hand on my shoulder. She can tell that I am upset by Jack's absence, but she probably thinks that I may know where he is and when he will be coming. James is smiling from ear to ear. He loves this stuff, where educators talk about kids who stand out and how it's through great opportunities, like this one, that we can get all kids to shine. Blah, blah, blah. The meal of Cornish hen, rice, and string bean almondine comes around and I want to hurl my plate across the room. I don't do that, however, because on the outside, I am in complete control of my faculties. Gramps is studying me. I catch his stare and he smiles. He knows something is up with me.

"Where is Jack, honey?" Mom asks me in a quiet voice.

"I don't know, Mom. I don't have my phone so I don't know what's up," I say. She smiles gently. She doesn't want me to harp on this.

Arlene is going on about how delicious the meal is.

"I can't remember the last time I had Cornish hen. It's a lovely change of pace, and cooked perfectly," she says.

Breck nods his head in agreement.

James is busy eating and smiling.

I just want to scream my head off.

The awards will now be presented. I am the first to be announced.

The man in the black suit with the white hair says my name, and everyone in the room claps for me. James holds up his iPhone and starts clicking in my face. Arlene is making noises, like "oh, there, there, how nice."

Mom is smiling and clapping. Then she is telling me to get up on the stage.

"Go, Lace. It's time for your speech, honey," Mom says. But I just look at her with a blank stare.

"Come on, honey, you can do this." I shake my head.

"I ripped up my speech, Mom. I don't have anything to say," I whisper. Mom looks like she has just seen an alien.

"You've got to go up there, Lace."

Mom is practically pushing me now. She pushes my elbow. It actually hurts.

"Ouch. You're hurting me, Mom," I say.

The clapping has quieted down. Everyone is looking at me. I am the girl in the black dress with the pink cardigan and the blank expression on my face.

James gets up and comes toward my seat. He gives me a warm smile, and acts like everything is fine. He takes a gentle hold on my shoulder and leads me to the stage. I go willingly. James leaves me at the stage. I take the three steps on my own.

I walk in slow motion to the center of the stage. There is a microphone. I remember they said to talk into the microphone.

"Hello," I say.

My voice sounds loud, but empty. Everyone is looking up at me.

I remember that Becky says I have to avoid being monotone.

"Um, thank you so much," I say, wiggling my voice up and down so that it definitely does not sound monotone.

I look over at Mom who looks like she might vomit.

"And thank you to my family for coming out, and to my guidance counselor, Ms. Gregory, who always reminds me that 'the future is now.'"

I gaze out at the tables of teachers and faculty and see Ms. Gregory. She is dressed in a tangerine colored dress. She is looking at me and smiling. She raises her fist to me in support.

I am busy trying to imagine everyone in the room naked. It is not doing anything for me.

"Um, I had a speech prepared, but this afternoon, I ripped it up because it sounded fake to me. It was about what I thought it should be about. That I dream of becoming a famous writer and that I want to travel and cover amazing stories, blah, blah, blah. But that's not even true."

I pause to look for Jack. He must be here, by now. No. Now what? What can I say? "The most important thing I know about writing is that if it's fake, it's garbage."

Right. So where can I possibly go with this? Where the hell is Jack? My feet hurt. Ms. Gregory is a moron.

"So how do I make it real? By being honest with myself, which is not always so easy." Something is coming from this little brain of mine. I'm just going to go with it.

"If I write about something that I don't really understand, it won't mean anything. When a writer writes, it has to be from her soul. If I am writing about pain, I have to know what it's like to have a sweet love snatched up from me. If I am writing about joy, I have to know how it feels to laugh from the belly, or see something magical, like an incredible sunset."

I pause to think about what I am saying. I can see my mother's eyes are looking especially moist.

"There is a lot I have to learn about writing, and I am looking forward to the journey. My biggest lesson, so far, is that good writers must be honest in their portrayal of the human condition. I am very appreciative of this award, and I promise to work hard, write every day, and keep my voice authentic. Thank you," I say.

As I walk away from the stage, my legs are wobbly. When I get to the table, I head straight for Gramps. He is whispering in my ear about how wonderful I am. Mom, James, Arlene, and Breck are congratulating me. I am crying a little. There is the sound of applause. Why couldn't Jack have been here?

Everyone is smiling and congratulating me for doing such a great job. Breck actually smiles at me and says, "Great speech."

It is difficult to sit there for another hour while the others accept their awards and make speeches. I am watching each person take the stage and make a speech, but I am not listening. I am sitting on the edge of my seat and I know that something is very wrong with Jack. I'm not sure what it is, but I know something has happened. As soon as the presentation is over, I tell Mom I need to leave.

"I'm going to go home and see if Jack is there," I say.

"Oh, all right sweetie. This has been some night. I am so proud of you, Lace."

I smile. I know she's proud, but right now, I am wondering if my boyfriend is alive.

I race out of the parking lot and try to stay as relaxed as possible while I am driving home. I still get a little nervous in the car at night, so I have to talk myself out of any bad feelings.

It will be all right. There's lots of explanations for this. Everything will be all right. I turn on my music and Jason Mraz is singing one of my old favorites: I'm Yours. I sing along and try to convince myself that everything will be all right.

When I reach my house, it takes me a moment to realize that the strange car in the driveway belongs to the babysitter. I forgot about her. When I get inside the house, Rosey is sleeping on the couch and does not want to be disturbed. The babysitter woman practically has her coat on. She can't wait to get out of there. Daisy is sleeping. I am rushing around trying to find my phone. I'm not sure where it is. I look in every room of the house, as the woman follows me, and tells me that her husband is expecting her by nine and it is a little after that, so can I just pay her so she can leave.

I am practically ignoring this woman, whose name is, Estelle or Adele. I don't really know. Her English is not so great, so I am a little confused about what she is asking, but I think she wants me to pay her so she can leave. The thing is, I have something bigger to take care of, and besides, I don't have enough money to pay her. The woman needs at least thirty bucks, and I know I only have a twenty. So, she is talking at me, and I am not even responding. I am on a mission to find my phone. I cannot stop to pay the babysitter.

In a last ditch effort, I decide to call my phone. It takes a few minutes for me to remember my number, but I finally do, because, I hear a ring tone. It's kind of low, but I still hear it. It rings three times, and then, darn, it goes to voice mail before I've had a chance to follow the sound. I call it again. I race to follow the sound. It takes me to, of all places, the nursery, where I have now succeeded in waking up Daisy, and I still can't find the phone.

Daisy's cries are fierce. She does not like to be awakened. But, clearly now, Estelle or Adele is off the clock and she won't do me any favors. I have to pick up Daisy and try my best to soothe her. The woman is talking again. Something about her husband and how she has to get home or he'll turn into a chicken. At least, that's what it sounds like.

I can tell that Daisy is not going to give me a break. She wants a diaper change and a bottle. Holding her and rocking her is not going to do it. If only I had my phone. If only Jack were here, instead of wherever he is. If only.

I take Daisy on a trip to the kitchen to warm her bottle. Then I go back to the nursery and give her a much-needed new diaper. I go back to the kitchen to get the bottle. Then, I go back to the nursery to sit in the rocking chair to give Daisy her bottle. All the while, the woman is going on about the husband and the chicken. I pretend that she is not there. I act like she is invisible. It is just me and Daisy and my anxiety bubbling out of control. As I sit in the rocking chair, I suddenly see it.

It's underneath the crib. A small black rectangle. My phone. I found my phone!

I take the bottle out of Daisy's mouth for just a fraction of a second so I can reach over and grab the phone. Daisy is not amused. How dare I do that to her? She shrieks.

"Please, Daisy, just one second."

Daisy is not happy. She gives me a look like, why are you so damned irresponsible about that phone? If I had a phone, I would never lose it.

But I know she would. Sometimes, no matter how careful you are, you lose it. That's just the way it goes. I reach for it. I have to really reach under the crib. Daisy is not entertained. Not even a little bit.

Estelle or Adele is getting louder and I know this is also upsetting my sister. "Please, can you keep it down?" I ask.

The woman's eye bulge out of her head. I can tell that she doesn't like me.

"My mother will be home in a few minutes and she will pay you, and then you can get back to your husband and the chicken," I say.

That's it. I am finished giving this woman my attention. I need to focus now. On my phone. Any messages? No. That's impossible. No voicemails. Two texts. OK. Two texts. That's going to be it. One text: **Good luck tonite.**

From August. Sent at 5:39. Second text: **You OK?**

From Becky at 9:12. Just a few minutes ago.

I text back: **No. Can't find Jack.**

Daisy is back on the bottle. Estelle or Adele has stopped talking to me. She is standing in the hallway.

I wait. I watch Daisy suck on the bottle, and then she stops. Her eyes close and she is falling back to sleep. I rock her ever so slightly. Go, girl.

Go to sleep. It's better in sleepy land. Just a few more baby sucks and then she is asleep. Slowly, carefully, I transfer her back into her crib. I close the door and stand outside to make sure she is really down.

Estelle or Adele gives me a dirty look.

I walk to the living room with my phone. The woman follows.

Through the living room window, I see headlights. It's either Jack or my mom. It's Mom and James. Good. They can deal with Estelle or Adele.

Mom walks in. She is carrying my certificate and the check that they gave me. Oops, I forgot about that. I just left it on the table. So, I am completely irresponsible. Daisy's right.

"Linda, how is everything?" Mom asks the babysitter. "Mom, this is Estelle, or is it Adele?" I ask.

"It's Linda," says the babysitter. She gives me a dirty look, and then turns back to smile at my mother.

"Your little girl was a pleasure," she says. I could punch that babysitter.

Mom and James are talking to Linda. James has his wallet in his hands, and he is making the motions to pay her.

I get a text: **I'm sure he's fine. Don't worry.**

I respond: **Holy Shit, Beck.**

I sit there. I don't know what to do. Mom and James are walking Estelle or Adele or Linda out of the house. Another car is coming in the drive. It's Breck, Arlene, and Gramps. Gramps. I almost forgot about him. They are expecting coffee. I forgot. I can't do this.

Arlene is carrying a large box in her hands. Gramps is holding Breck for support as they walk up to the front door. Rosey is waking up and barking up a storm. Please don't let it wake up Daisy.

When they come in the house, everyone is smiling, even Breck. Arlene puts the box down on the kitchen table and asks me to open it. Inside is a beautiful vanilla cake with pink icing that reads: Congrats to the writer!

It's so sweet of all of them to make such a fuss over me. Mom puts her arm on my back and asks if she can speak to me in the other room. I follow her into her bedroom.

She closes the door, sits on the bed, takes off her heels, and says, "Come here." I sit on the bed.

"Where is he?" she asks.

"I don't know. He said he would be there."

"Shit," Mom says. She pulls off her sweater. She's is wearing a white bra, and it is wet where her boobs are. Gross. She hunts for her black sweat suit on the love seat and puts it on.

"Let's stay calm. Do you want James to go look for him? He could just make sure that he's safe, you know?" Mom asks.

I am a bit thrown by Mom's compassion. I forget for a second that I don't have to hide my true feelings. I can let it all hang out.

"I don't know, Mom."

"Well, how about we get comfy, and we'll have coffee and cake and just relax until we hear something?"

"OK, sounds good," I say.

I go into my room, which is really Gramps' room now and I throw off my dress and heels. I put on some raggy sweats and a black T-shirt. I wash my face in the bathroom and look at myself in the mirror. The diamond wishbone necklace is glistening. I put my fingers over it and make a wish. Please let Jack be all right.

In the kitchen, the cake is out and there's coffee and milk set up. Arlene is putting out plates. Breck is sitting at the table, looking sullen. James sees me and gives me a big smile. Gramps is playing with Rosey-O in the living room.

Breathe. I just have to breathe. I am contemplating calling Jack's house, but I really don't know if I can bear talking to Julie. I am going to give myself until 10:00 and then decide if I should call her to casually ask her if she knows where Jack might be, and why he might have missed the awards dinner.

I serve myself a huge piece of cake. It is so sweet and sugary, it's almost sickening. Everyone has a piece, even Mom, who has been dieting lately.

"This was a really special night, Lace," Mom says. It's hard because she knows I'm losing my mind over Jack, but she is still so proud and happy about the speech and the award.

"How did you come up with that speech, dear?" Arlene asks.

I shrug my shoulders. "I really don't know. I wasn't sure what I was going to say. I just knew

that I couldn't read the speech that I had written a few days ago. That was so phony and fake," I say.

Then James stands. He looks at me and raises his cup of coffee. What's going on?

"I would like to say something," he says. Everyone looks at him with curiosity.

"I came into Lace's life abruptly. At first, I didn't think she liked me very much." Oh my God. Where is this going? Can this night be any worse?

"But I tried to give her the space that she needed and the space that she deserved. I was so happy when she got closer to Kate. Then we had Daisy girl. And now it feels like we are a family. I feel really close to you, Lace. I can count on you. I want you to know that you can always count on me. I am very proud of you. To Lacey, a beautiful young writer with a very promising future," he says.

Holy shit.

Everyone smiles.

Everyone raises their coffee cups. Gramps manages to spill his all over the table. Mom just laughs. She is on such a high. Even Breck has broken into a smile.

"Thanks, James. Right back at you!" I say, because I don't know what else I could possibly say. James is such a nice guy, and sometimes, I just don't know how to deal with it.

It's past ten and I just can't call Julie. I just can't do it.

We are in the living room playing charades. It's my turn. I have to act out the movie Spiderman. I am trying to creep up a building. Then I try to weave a web.

"Climbing the stairs," Arlene guesses.

"That's not a movie, Arlene," Breck says. "The Hunger Games" Gramps guesses.

I shake my head. I try to act spidery, but it is no use. It's not working.

Then I try to land on a surface and I throw out my arms as if they have a silk thread that I secure in the ground.

James yells at the top of his lungs, "Spiderman!"

"Yes, yes," I say. "Finally."

I am a little relieved. I look around and Mom is almost asleep on Gramps. Arlene looks like she is next and Breck is yawning. It's eleven on a school night. No sign of Jack.

Arlene and Breck go back to the hotel. They will be back in the morning to spend the day. Mom and James go to bed. Gramps sits with me on the couch.

He doesn't say anything. He doesn't have to. He knows that something is up with Jack. He also knows that if I wanted to talk about it, I would. I sit next to him and we pet Rosey. I am almost asleep when I hear a thud.

"What was that?" I say. Gramps shakes his head.

"Not sure I heard anything there, Lace."

I stand up and look out the living room window. I don't see anything. It's probably my imagination.

There's a pounding noise. It's coming from the kitchen. "I'll go, Gramps. Maybe it's Jack."

Gramps nods.

I rush into the kitchen. I see a shadowy figure at the door. It's Jack. "Jack?"

"What's up?" he asks.

He's not right. His face is messed up. He has a cut on his head and he's got dried blood in his hair.

"Oh my God! What happened? Are you all right?" I ask. I open the door for him to come in, but he won't come in. He just stays outside.

"Come in," I say.

"No, I'm good," he says.

His body is stiff like a statue.

"Are you all right?" I ask. "What happened to your face? You're bleeding."

"Oh, I'm all right. Are you all right?" he asks. He's slurring his words.

I am confused. Who is this person? "Jack, what is going on with you?" I ask.

"I think I need to ask you that same question. I thought I knew you, Lace. I thought you were the one," he says.

"Jack, you're a mess. What are you saying?" I say.

"No! You don't have the right to ask me what I'm doing. You need to come clean," he shouts. I can hear Gramps and Rosey coming into the kitchen. I don't know what to do.

"Jack, is that you?" Gramps asks. He comes to the door and looks at Jack. "What's happened to you?" Gramps asks.

Jack doesn't say anything. He gives Gramps a blank stare. "Are you drunk? Did you get into a fight?" Gramps asks. "Maybe," answers Jack.

"Maybe you should come inside. Lacey will make some coffee. We can talk. Everything will be all right." Gramps says, reaching his hand out for Jack.

"No. That is not going to work for me," Jack says. He runs his hands through his hair. His button down shirt is filthy, and his dress slacks are stained and wrinkled.

"Are you driving a car, boy?" Gramps says. Jack shakes his head no.

Rosey comes toward Jack and starts sniffing.

Gramps picks up Rosey. "Rosey doesn't like drunks," Gramps says. "Gramps, that's so mean," I say.

I give Gramps a desperate look. Please don't do anything to upset Jack any more than he already is.

"Sometimes you have to be cruel to be kind. Shakespeare said that. If he's drinking, Lacey, he's no good to anyone."

Gramps turns around and walks out of the kitchen.

"I'll be in the living room if you need me, Lacey" he says.

"Are you? Are you drinking, Jack?" I ask.

"Who wants to know?" he asks.

He looks like a little boy. In the dark, I think he could pass for a ten year old boy. "I want to know. Me. Your girlfriend."

"Maybe. That's all I'm saying. Now you need to do the talking. All I know is, I was on my way to the florist to get flowers for you for your big night."

He stops talking for a minute. He takes out a flask from his pocket and takes a big gulp. He holds it toward me. Almost sticks it in my face.

"Want some?" he teases. "No. I don't drink," I say.

"Miss Goody Two Shoes, huh?" he asks. Ouch.

"So, what happened, Jack? You went to get flowers and what?" I shout. What the hell is wrong with Jack? This isn't my Jack.

I walk outside so that we are both standing on the stoop by the kitchen door, under the light.

"So, I run into that girl you know, August. I tell her I'm getting flowers for you and she tells me that she's so glad that the two of us are back together because we make such a good pair. And, I'm thinking, what the fuck, there's something that this girl is hiding, this August. This month girl," Jack says. It's kind of hard to understand what he is saying because he is slurring his words.

He stops to drink more. His face is wild. He looks like he's half human and half wolf.

Something terrible is going to happen. I just know it. What the hell did August say? I never should have trusted her. She's so weird with her high-fives.

"So, I say, well, we were never really apart. I just had to go away for a while," Jack explains. I nod my head.

"Right?" I say. Come on spit it out.

"But then April, May, June, July, August, whatever the fuck, says, 'with everything that poor Lacey went through, I'm just glad you're here now,'" he says.

Jack looks at me. I look down.

"With everything that poor Lacey went through," he repeats.

I can smell the alcohol. He also smells like blood and sweat. He is quiet for a minute. I try to take hold of his hand, but he pulls away.

"You were pregnant?" he asks, in a very soft voice, his eyes burning through mine. I don't say anything. I don't move. Please make this all right. Please God. Fix this.

"You were going to have my baby, and you didn't tell me?" he says.

"Maybe it wasn't my baby?" Jack says, his voice cracking on the word baby.

"What! That's crazy. There's only you. You were and are the only one," I say. I reach for him, but he pushes me away.

"So, what about this secret relationship you have? What's going on there, Lacey?" he asks. "What are you talking about, Jack? You are really scaring me."

"Oh, I don't want to scare you, Lace. No. I wouldn't want to do that," Jack, says in a mocking tone. There is something crazy in Jack's eyes.

"You and Mason Cleets are friends? Isn't that nice? That guy is such an asshole. You have a "special thing" with him," Jack says, sarcasm and anger oozing out of him.

"What? Who told you that?" I ask.

"Well, first that month girl told me that. Then I went and asked Mason for myself."

"You did?" I gasp.

"I did. I also punched that dick right in the face."

"You punched Mason?" I ask. So that's why Mason wasn't at the awards presentation tonight. "Why? Mason is just a kid who I drank coffee with at Starbucks," I say. "It was totally innocent."

"Oh yeah? That's what we did. That's how we met. That's how this all started. Over coffee at Starbucks. Don't you remember? " he asks. His face is in my face, but there's just anger there.

"Calm down. You are letting your imagination get the best of you," I say. "August had no right to tell you anything. She's just a big-mouth loser," I say.

My tears have started. Why didn't I tell Jack all of this? "Don't cry. You don't have the right to cry."

"Why?" I ask.

"Because you weren't honest with me. Because you hurt me. And because we are done." I am horrified. I am frozen. Did he just say that? This cannot be happening.

"Jack, please let me explain. You weren't here. I didn't know what was going on with me, or why I felt so bad. I thought it was just a broken heart. I couldn't stand the smell of coffee. I thought that it was because that's how we met. I was so lost without you."

Jack just stares at me.

"My mom told me that she was pregnant. A few days later I started to wonder if that's what was happening to me. I didn't think it was possible because we used a condom," I said.

"That's right, Lace. We did," Jack nods.

"But I took the test and it said pregnant. I went out with August to get some air, and I stupidly told her what was going on with me, with us. I had to tell someone."

"You told her you were pregnant, but you didn't tell me. Don't you see something is wrong with that? Very wrong. Fucked up wrong," he says. His face is so close to mine. But he is not going to kiss me. He looks like he is disgusted, like he might spit in my face.

"Please, just listen to me. I didn't know what I was doing. You were gone, and you stopped all communications with me. Just stopped. I didn't know what to do. I didn't want to interfere with your rehab. I wanted what was best for you," I said.

"You think you know what's best for me? You think you can pick and choose what you decide to tell me? Just tell me the happy stuff and leave out the sad stuff? Leave out the details of a pregnancy that went bad? Leave out the details of you lying in bed in your own blood?" he asks.

"Who told you that?" I ask. August didn't know that. "Mason. My great buddy, Mase. He told me that."

"I never told him that," I said. But then I remembered that I let him read my writing and I had written all about the blood in the bed and how I didn't know if I was dying or not, and how I only tried to save myself to save the baby.

"You told Mason that, but you didn't tell me. You say you love me. That doesn't feel like love, Lace. It feels like deceit. I don't want that. I can't handle that," he says.

He sits on the stoop and buries his head in his hands.

I sit and lean into him. I rub my face in his hair. He pushes away. "I love you, Jack. Please forgive me for not telling you," I say.

But he just ignores me. It's like I'm not even there.

He gets up and takes a few steps away from the house. Then he turns to face me.

"Make sure you let Gramps know that I am not driving. He doesn't have to worry," he says.

And then Jack drinks again. He looks up to the sky as he drinks. He drinks and drinks, and then he falls backward onto the grass. It looks as if he has fallen asleep.

I call out his name, but he doesn't respond. I scream.

"Jack!"

I don't know what the hell is happening. I look down at him. He looks so peaceful. So young. I try to wake him. I shake him. "Jack," I scream. He doesn't move. I shake his head. I shake his hands. "Come on, Jack!"

Nothing.

I scream for Gramps. I scream for Mom.

Gramps comes outside. Rosey is behind him. Gramps gets on his knees and tries to wake up Jack.

"Come on, fella, wake up. Jack? Can you hear me?" Gramps shouts. Mom and James rush outside.

"James is calling an ambulance," Mom shouts.

I am hysterical. My mom, in her nightgown, is holding me as I sit on the ground next to Jack.

"I did this, Mommy. I did this to Jack. I didn't tell him about the baby. I didn't tell him the truth. I made him drink again. And now look at him," I say, as I cry like a baby.

Mom rocks me back and forth. She lets me cry and say whatever I want to. "I've lost him," I say.

Gramps goes inside the house to check on Daisy. James is waiting by the street for the ambulance.

“This is the worst day of my life,” I say.

James is signaling the ambulance. Holy crap. This is real.

CHAPTER EIGHT

Living in a Jackless World

Jack is taken to the hospital in an ambulance. Just like that. The ambulance drives away. I'm holding my hands up and shrugging my shoulders. What the hell was that? What just happened? How did I lose him?

We are standing in front of the house. My mom is in her nightgown. She is hugging me, as I cry into her neck. James says he will take me to the hospital. Do I want to go?

Of course I want to go. I have to make sure that he is all right, before I step out of his life. I am shivering now. Mom is patting my back and telling me to breathe.

She walks me to the car. James is behind the wheel, warming up the car.

"Just breathe. Breathe. I'll say a prayer for him, Lace. That's what I'll do now. While you and James are at the hospital."

She helps me into the car. I feel like I will never stop crying. I try to speak, but my voice is hoarse.

"Mom, will you call Jack's mother, Julie? Will you tell her what's happening? Please don't make me call her. She's so cold. She will definitely blame this on me," I say.

Mom nods. "Of course. I'll go inside and call her right now."

James drives to the hospital. We don't talk. He doesn't even try to say anything, and I appreciate that. We park in the emergency area, and I think how ironic to be coming here once again. First, I was here because I was pregnant and something was horribly wrong with the baby. Then, I was back here when Mom was having Daisy. And then I was back again with Jack, when Gramps fell. And now, I am here again. For Jack.

We are directed to the seating area in the emergency room. A nurse says that Jack is being examined. James and I sit next to each other in silence. After about ten minutes, I see Julie and John, Jack's parents, rushing to the nurse's station. A nurse is leading them down a hallway.

They are with Jack. I want to be there, but he doesn't want me there, and I know that it is wrong to force myself on him. We wait another half an hour and then James goes to the nurse's station to get a report.

He comes back a few minutes later to tell me that Jack has alcohol poisoning.

"What is that? I mean, I know it means he's had too much to drink, but what happens?" I ask, frantically.

"It's when the person drinks large amounts of alcohol in a short period of time."

"Will he be all right?" I ask.

"I really don't know," says James. "We just have to wait and see what happens. The nurse is going to let us know. She promised. That one," James points to the nurse's station.

"The tall one with the blonde braids. She promised to come and tell us when there is news."

"Oh my God," I say.

James texts my mom to tell her that we are not sure what's happening yet.

I shut my eyes and I can remember Jack on the ground. Not moving. Not looking alive.

"I just wish I could fix him. He's just got that one little problem. He just doesn't know when to quit," I say.

James nods. "I know someone like him. You know that. Breck never knew when to quit."

"Is he going to die?" I ask.

James shakes his head. "I hope not."

"What's going to happen to him, James?" I ask.

James shrugs his shoulders. "I don't know. It took my dad years to quit."

"Jack is so strong in every other way. How can he let this ruin him?"

"It's complicated. I'm sure he wants to stop. It's more than just mind over matter. He's physically addicted. It's a powerful thing," James says.

James gets up and asks if I want something to drink from the vending machine. A bottle of water would be good. He comes back in a few minutes. He hands me the water and sits by my side.

"I think I heard the nurse say that they are pumping his stomach," James says. "Oh my God. Poor Jack. I'll bet that really hurts, but at least he's alive." This is so awful.

"It's probably a good sign in some way. Like once they get the alcohol out, he'll be better," James offers.

We sit in silence. Then I have an idea. I can go to the hospital chapel. Say a prayer. Maybe it will help. So that's what I do. I tell James I'll be back soon. He doesn't ask where I'm going, he just gives me a nod.

In the chapel, it is quiet, clean, and empty.

I sit near a statue of a cross and I close my eyes and tell God how sorry I am for not being a better person. I tell him that I know I am asking him once again for his help. I beg him to take care of Jack. I plead with God to help Jack find the strength to stop drinking so that he doesn't kill himself, or ruin his life. I make a deal with God. If he takes care of him, I will let him go.

I go back to James, who has his eyes closed. "Anything?" I ask.

"Well, I asked the blond nurse if she knew anything. She said that the treatment required Jack to be on breathing support and intravenous. He needs fluids and vitamins to replace all that was lost in the body," he says quietly.

"How horrible. I just wish I could be with him," I say. "Do you want to try to see him?"

I cry. I don't think that's what they want now. If Jack knows that I'm in the room, he might get more upset. I don't want that.

I shake my head no.

"I think it's best if we just stay where we are," I say. James nods.

I must have fallen asleep. The next thing I know, the blonde nurse is standing over us. "James? James?" she is saying.

James opens his eyes. He stands at attention. "What is it? What's going on?" he asks.

The blond nurse smiles. She looks at me.

"Your friend is going to be all right. We pumped his stomach so he is really sore now and weak, but he is conscious."

"Will he be all right?" I ask.

"I think so. He's responding well. His parents are with him." I nod.

"I'm so glad."

"Let me tell you something," the nurse says. I look at her with curiosity.

"You saved his life. If you hadn't been there, there's a good chance that he might not have made it. A lot of alcohol poisoning victims end up choking on their vomit, or worse. You did a good thing by getting him here," she says.

I nod.

"You're a good friend. He will know that. I will make sure I let him know that," she says. "Thanks," I say. The word friend is stinging.

I turn to James. "We can go now," I say. "Are you sure, Lace?"

I nod. "He doesn't want to see me," I say. "He broke up with me. Because I am a liar," I say.

"Thank you for everything you've said," I tell the nurse. She nods and puts her hands on my hands.

"May I call in the morning to make sure that he is all right?" I ask.

"Of course," she says. "My name is Natalie and I get off at nine. Ask for me and I'll give you an update."

I nod.

"Go home and get some sleep," she says. James and I walk out of the hospital.

I feel bad that I haven't said anything to Julie and John. Did they expect me to tell them what happened? I just can't face them. I just feel like Julie would like to blame this all on me.

As we get into the car, I see that it is after two in the morning. "I'm so sorry about this whole thing, James."

"Don't worry about it," he says.

"All this drama. This is way more than you signed on for," I say.

"Don't talk that way. Listen, just for the record, you didn't lie. You are not a liar. You made an omission. You didn't know how to tell him about the pregnancy. You didn't think about it from his perspective. But that doesn't make you a liar, or a bad person," James says. "Give him some time and he'll see it that way."

But I can't help the way I feel. I brought this on myself. I deserve this. This is my punishment for not being open and honest. If only I had told him everything that had happened to me. Why didn't I?

I do not sleep at all. I hold Rosey all night. She licks away my tears. In the morning, I call Natalie, who tells me that Jack is doing all right. He is drinking liquids and slowly gaining his strength. His family is sitting with him, and they are making plans for some kind of intervention. I thank her for the report. When Arlene and Breck come over, I ask to speak to Breck alone. I tell him I have to walk Rosey and I ask him to come along. He takes the leash and walks outside with me.

It's cold. Breck puts his collar up and wraps a scarf around his neck. I am too numb to be cold. "You all right?" he asks. "Your eyes are all puffy."

We walk down the street. I don't say anything for a minute. I am trying to prevent myself from crying. I am breathing deeply. Breck looks concerned and he stops and looks at me.

"What is it? Is it Jack?" he asks.

I nod.

"I knew something was up when he didn't show up last night. What can I do?" he asks. I knew that somewhere deep inside, Breck was a really nice man.

"He was drinking last night. He's in the hospital. Alcohol poisoning."

Breck nods. "Oh no."

I start to cry.

"Breck, it's all my fault," I say.

"It can't be, Lacey. We all have to take responsibility for ourselves."

I shake my head. "You don't understand. I did this to him. I tried to hide something from him. Something horrible. Last night, before the awards presentation, he found out the truth and he lost it. It's all my fault."

Breck grabs hold of my hand.

"No. That just isn't true. Nobody makes another person drink." Rosey stops to do her business.

"Take me to the hospital. Let me talk to him," Breck says. "Maybe I can help him."

After I put Rosey back in the house, I tell my mom what's going on. She thinks it's a good idea for Breck to talk to Jack. She says James has told her how many people he's helped with their drinking problems.

I drop Breck off at the entrance of the hospital. I give him my cell number and tell him that I can pick him up whenever he is ready to leave. Breck nods.

Then I ask Breck to give Jack a message for me. "Sure, what's the message?"

"Tell him that I love him, and I that never meant to hurt him." Breck nods and shuts the car door.

I nod off on the couch for a while. When I wake up, Mom is next to me. She feeds me toast. She tells me about her conversation with Julie last night.

"She thanked me for calling her, but she was pretty cold. Distant."

"I'm not surprised. That's how she is. Or, maybe she is just that way with me," I say.

"But she said thank you for calling the ambulance and not to worry about Jack. She was finally going to give him the care that he needed."

So she gets to nurse him back to health. That cold woman.

Breck returns to the house at about three in the afternoon. He has taken a taxi from the hospital. He pats me on the back, and gives me a soft smile.

"He'll be all right," he says.

"Did you give him my message?"

Breck nods. "I did, but right now, he needs help. He says he'll call you in a few days to talk."

I feel relieved that he didn't say he doesn't want to ever see me again. But I feel sad because I know I have lost him. Maybe I never really had him.

Several hours later, Mom and James have greeted a nice babysitter (not Estelle or whatever her name is), and we are all headed to the city for a fancy dinner. Mom was going to cancel under the circumstances, but I didn't think that was right. I am in the back seat of the SUV sitting next to Arlene. Gramps and Breck are behind us. I am trying to be in the moment. I am trying not to think of my broken heart. On the outside, I am succeeding. On the inside, I am dying.

It is a full week before I hear from Jack again. He calls me and asks to meet for coffee at Starbucks. It's a Sunday morning and there is a hint of spring in the air. I think that's nice. Spring can mean a fresh start, a new beginning.

When I get there, Jack is already at the back table with two cups in front of him. I walk toward him and he smiles.

"Jack," I say. "How are you?" I reach over to kiss him, and he gives me his cheek. I'm disappointed.

"Hey, Lace. Here's your coffee."

"Thanks. Is it decaf?" Jack nods.

I sit down. Jack looks tired, but he looks better than he did a few days ago. The wounds on his head have almost healed and his coloring is back. His hair is cut very short.

"How are you feeling?" I ask. "I'm doing all right."

"I was so worried," I say.

"Listen, I wanted to tell you how sorry I am. I know what happened wasn't your fault. I didn't deal with any of it very well. I just got so paranoid. I didn't know how to control my thoughts," he says.

He looks down at the table. He won't meet my eyes.

"Jack?" I ask. "Are you leaving again?"

He nods. "I'll finish my senior year in California. It will be easier without the distractions. Uncle Aiden is working his tail off to get me back into that school and out of this one."

"Am I a distraction?" I ask.

He is still looking down at the table. "Can't you look at me?" I ask.

He shakes his head.

"I'm sorry," Jack whispers.

We have sat at this table so many times before. I would be practically sitting on his lap and Jack would be feeding pieces of cookie to me. We'd laugh and flirt, and in between taking sips of coffee, we'd kiss. Good times.

"I'll be in touch through Breck. He'll let you know how I am doing. Lace, he's a really good guy."

I'm glad about that.

"Do you forgive me, Jack?"

I knew I shouldn't have worn eye makeup. Tears are streaming down my face. I take a napkin and blow my nose.

"I'm a mess," I say.

"No, you're not a mess, Lace. I'm a mess."

"I don't care," I say. "If I can't have you in my life, I don't know what will happen to me," I say.

Jack reaches across the small, round table to take my hand. I squeeze it. I squeeze it really tight. I want him to feel my love.

"You saved my life. I know that. Thank you, Lacey."

I shake my head. I don't want any credit for that. I just want Jack. "Let's just rewind. Take it back to when we first met," I say.

"Lacey, listen to me. You will be fine. I thought that I had this problem covered, but I don't and I can't take you down with me. That isn't fair, Lace. I don't know what will happen. I know I love you. I will always love you, Lacey," Jack says.

"Are we not together anymore?" I ask.

"I can't make a promise to you that I may not be able to keep. I can't do that," Jack says.

Up until now, he hasn't had any of his coffee. I can see the steam coming from the cup. He takes a big gulp.

Oh my God. I am losing him again. This is the only boy that I have ever loved. I can't imagine loving anyone else.

If anyone is looking at us, they are really getting a show. I am crying and I don't want to ever let go of his hand. We just sit like that for the longest time.

"Please, Jack, I say, please don't hate me for not telling you about what happened. I was afraid. I was so happy when you came back to me, and I just didn't want to go back to that dark place. It was such a bad time," I say.

He nods. "I know."

"Jack?" I say.

"Lacey, I could never hate you. You make me feel like it's possible to be this strong person, who doesn't need the crutch of alcohol. Everything I do, I do for you, even if I'm not with you."

Jack lets go of my hand. He stands, and I stand. One last embrace. He puts his arms around me and I can smell that familiar Jack smell. I want to get lost in his arms. But the hug is too brief. He releases me abruptly. He looks deep into my eyes, and tries to give me a smile, but it doesn't quite work. It doesn't stay on his face. He whispers into my ear, "I love you." Then he is gone.

I am Jackless again.

Two days after meeting up with Jack, there's a bad story floating around. It seems that Jack went to church with his mother, but he was drunk. He began arguing with her while the sermon was being delivered. Jack was asked to leave the church. It was quite a scene. His mother was crushed. Her perfect son had humiliated her. August called me and wanted to be the first to share the details. I told her I had to go. I'm done with her.

Uncle Aiden has taken Jack back to California. That was a few weeks ago. I haven't heard anything else and I don't expect to. I have to pretend that Jack doesn't exist. It's the only way I can move on.

CHAPTER NINE

One year and several months later

Life Happens

"I refuse to go to the prom. I just don't see any point in it," I say with my hands folded across my chest.

"Why not?" asks Becky, her hands waving in the air, as she blows her just-polished hands dry. "Because I just don't like anyone except for you, Beck," I say.

And I really feel that way. I'm happy to be graduating high school, and I've had a great time in school, but I don't want to go to prom. Does that make me weird? I don't care.

Rosey barks and shifts from one side of my lap to the other. Daisy is pounding on a drum, and it's so loud, I can't hear myself think.

"Stop!" I shout. I put my hands over my ears.

"Daisy, why do you like all the loud toys? Can't you play with something more quiet, like this little baby doll?"

I hand Daisy the doll, but first I show her how to hold the baby and rock her. Daisy tries it.

"Very good. See, Daisy? Isn't that more fun than a loud drum?" Daisy toddles away with the baby doll in her arms.

"Isn't that sweet? What a good mommy Daisy is," I say.

Just when I think Daisy is going to agree with me, she throws baby to the ground and resumes her drum-playing.

"Did she really just do that?" I ask Becky.

"Oh yes she did. She's headstrong, just like her big sister." I laugh. Becky has a point.

"Becky, we used to love playing with dolls, didn't we?" I ask.

"Yep, but we weren't as young as Daisy, and I think it was Barbie dolls and we took turns dressing up the dolls in sexy outfits," Becky says. "Which may not have been the best use of our time."

I think about what Becky is saying and I realize she's totally right.

"Daisy likes the fact that she can make noise with the drum," Becky points out.

"You are definitely going to be a child psychologist. I would put money down on that," I say.

"Probably, but you are changing the subject," Becky says.

"Yes, I am," I say. "Headstrong," says Becky.

Becky grabs a bunch of chips from the chip bowl on the coffee table and shoves them down her throat.

"Can't you even wait until your nails dry," I say. "Sheesh, what an animal!" Becky is crunching and munching, and staring at me.

"What?" I say.

"I know what it is," she says. "What?" I ask.

Something tells me Becky is about to get heavy on me. She has that look. "Look, I know you don't want to go if you can't go with him," she says. "Who?" I play dumb.

"Jack. Jack. Jack. You know that's who we are talking about," she says.

I glare at her. How can she bring up his name? We have an agreement not to bring up his name.

"I get it. You went to his formal and nothing can top that and now it doesn't make sense to go to your prom with some guy that means nothing to you," Becky explains.

I nod. That's exactly it.

"Did you ever think of calling Jack and asking him if he would go with you?" Becky asks.

"Becky, are you out of your mind? I haven't spoken to Jack in a year. We know some details about each other's lives thanks to Breck, but that's it," I explain.

"I don't get that," Becky makes a long and loud burp.

"Gross, Becky!" I say.

Daisy tries to imitate me. "Goss, Becky!" We all laugh.

"It's just, I know how much you still love him, and I am betting that he still loves you," she says. "Yes, but, chances are, he's either moved on, or he hasn't--" I stammer.

"Hasn't what?" asks Becky.

"Hasn't been able to stop drinking," I say quietly. "Oh," says Becky. "Forgot about that for a minute."

We're both silent for a bit. I watch Daisy as she sucks the tip of her drum stick. I trade her a cracker for the drum stick, and she happily accepts it. Then Rosey starts begging for a cracker.

"These guys are getting hungry for dinner," I say. "Yep, where's Kate?" Becky asks.

"Mom and James went for coffee. Isn't that so cute?" I ask.

"Adorable. But, does that mean you have to make dinner for you and Daisy?" Becky asks.

"No, I'm sure they will be back soon," I smile, and gaze out the window and watch the sky darken.

"Anyway, Becky, you are going to have a really great time with Hoff, and you shouldn't feel bad for me in anyway. If I wanted to go, I would go. You know that."

Becky nods.

"I just feel guilty having fun without you," says Becky.

"That's crazy, Beck. If I went, I wouldn't have fun. Why should I ruin your fun?" I say.

"I just wish I could find a dress. Everything is so ugly. I finally get to go to prom and now everything is hideous," she says. "That's my luck."

And just then I have an idea. I remember how much Becky loved the pink lace dress that I wore to Jack's semi-formal. It's just hanging in my closet.

"Hey Beck," I say.

"Yes?" she turns to me. She's got chips and cracker crumbs all over her face. I just have to laugh.

"What?" she says, smiling. "You know, soon I will be in Boston, and you will be in Manhattan or Vermont, and you will miss me, Lacey. You won't be able to make fun of me."

"You're right, Beck. As usual," I say.

"War right Veck," says Daisy. "As use-al."

Daisy is so proud of herself because she can repeat what other people are saying. "Silly girl," I say.

Daisy is all smiles.

"I've got just the dress for you," I say.

"Oh, really? Tell me?" she asks.

"The one that I wore to Jack's formal. Remember it?"

"Remember it? It was only the most gorgeous dress in the entire world. I have the back of the dress stuck in my memory. Sexy open back and the drape. Sublime!"

I laugh.

"Let me get it and you can try it on," I say, gently pushing Rosey off my lap so I can get up from the couch.

"But, that gown is too perfect. It's too nice for me. What if I spill something on it?" she says. "So, you get it dry-cleaned," I say.

"But what about the fact that I'm like four feet taller than you?" she asks.

"It could be like the *Sisterhood of the Traveling Pants*. Remember, how each girl wore the pants even though they were different sizes? And, each girl looked awesome?" I ask.

Becky nods. "Best book ever!" she says.

"You will probably have to wear pink ballet flats to make it work. What do you think?" I ask.

"I think you are the sweetest friend in the world and I love you. If I didn't love Hoff so much, I would ask you to the prom as my date," she says.

"That's OK, Beck," I say. "Just keep an eye on Daisy while I get it out of my closet," I say.

"No prob. Come here, Daisy, let's play," Becky stands up and picks up Daisy, who is looking awfully tired all of a sudden.

"You may want to close your eyes for a bit, Miss Daisy," I say to my sister. "No!" says Daisy. "No close eyes!"

No surprise there. Daisy hates taking naps. She's afraid that she will miss something. "OK," I say. "No nap for Daisy."

It is covered in plastic paper. When I unwrap the dress, it seems to tug at my heartstrings. It was such a perfect dress for a girl named Lacey, who was so in love with her perfect boy named Jack. That seems so long ago. I study the material and touch it with my fingertips. I can remember standing in the dress and feeling like a princess. When I arrived at Jack's pre-prom party, everyone looked at me like I was the most beautiful thing on the planet. When Jack saw me, it looked like his eyes were going to pop out of his head. And when I turned around for him and he saw the revealing back of the dress, he looked at me in such a way, all I could do was blush.

Jack. I miss you. Wherever you are and whatever you are doing, know that I miss you.

When I return to the family room with the dress, Daisy has her head resting on Becky's shoulder. Becky picks Daisy up and starts dancing around the room. The motion seems to put Daisy to sleep. Becky looks at me and smiles. I put my finger to my lips and we both wait quietly for Daisy to fall out.

It doesn't take too long, maybe ten minutes. Becky gently lays Daisy on the couch and we cover her up with a blanket and Rosey nestles under Daisy's neck. Becky goes into the other room to try on the dress. When she returns, she takes my breath away.

She is a vision. The dress comes down to her ankles, but it looks like it is the perfect length. The pale pink compliments Becky's light skin and hair.

"You're radiant," I whisper. Becky nods.

"It's too beautiful for words, Lacey. I don't know if I can really borrow it," she says. "Why not?" I ask.

"I just don't know if it's right to wear something that means so much to you. I know how much you loved wearing it and being with Jack. I know how much Jack loved you in it," she said.

"It doesn't take any of that away from me. I still have that."

"Are you sure?" Becky begins to cry.

"I'm sure, Beck. You look awesome. Wait until Hoff sees you in it."

Beck slowly turns for me and the back of the dress really is a work of art. Then Becky takes off the dress and we wrap it back up in the plastic. Becky hugs me and tells me that I am her very best friend and that she will always love me, no matter what. I am happy to have made her so happy. After she leaves, I push the coffee table next to the couch so Daisy can't fall. Then I go into my room while Daisy sleeps.

My bed is unmade and I can't remember the last time it was made. I decide that now is as good a time as any to turn over a new leaf and try to keep my room clean. So I begin the long and involved process of cleaning up the piles of dirty clothes and clean clothes that cover the floor.

For a few minutes, I am unstoppable. I have thrown dirty clothes in the hamper, hung up clean clothes, made the bed, put away books and shoes, and tossed old papers and magazines. But then, all of a sudden, I am stuck when I catch a glimpse of him in the photo he gave me last Christmas. I feel a stinging in my heart. Gramps.

I would gladly give up this room and go back to sleeping on the couch if I could just have him back for another day. I miss him so much. And when I look down, I see Rosey at my feet. She misses him, too. She really does. After he died, she just sat by the door waiting for him to come home. No matter how many times I told her that he wasn't coming back, she wouldn't leave the space. About two days later, she started spending a few hours at a time on the bed. But then she would still return to the door. It broke my heart.

Gramps died in his sleep three months ago in late February. I was trying to wake him up to ask him if he wanted me to make him French toast. When he didn't wake up, I started screaming. I really scared Daisy. Rosey had no idea anything was wrong. She was sleeping next to him.

In some ways, it was a relief. Gramps was becoming feeble. There were times when he didn't know if he was coming or going. He seemed angry a lot of the time. And, he really gave Mom a hard time. He really knew how to push her buttons. But he was the closest thing I had to a father as a child. I loved him. Dear old Gramps.

I can hear Daisy talking now. These days, her naps never last more than twenty minutes. Mom calls them power naps.

"Lacey. Where Lacey?" she calls.

"I'm coming!" I say.

As I race into the family room, I see her sitting up on the couch with the baby doll on her lap. "Daisy," I say. "Hey you!"

Daisy beams. "Hey Lacey," she says.

And just like that, I go from being filled with grief, to being filled with happy thoughts. Daisy can do that to me.

After a few minutes of playing with the baby doll, I see headlights turning into the drive way. "Guess whose home?" I say to Daisy.

"Daddy?" I nod.

"Mommy?" I nod.

As Mom and James burst into the house, Daisy jumps for joy. I have this thought that if Gramps were here, he'd probably get mad that we were fussing over Daisy, and not giving enough attention to Rosey. So I scoop Rosey up and give her some love, and I know this would make my Gramps happy.

James takes Daisy in his arms. "What's up?" I say.

Mom is smiling from ear to ear. If I didn't know better, I'd think she had a secret. "Ladies, we have news!" exclaims James.

"News. News," Daisy cries out. "Mom, what's going on?" I ask.

Mom places her hand on her belly and says, "Guess what?" I'm not sure I like where this is going.

"It's official!" James shouts. "We're pregnant!" Mom says.

And just then, Mom comes rushing to me with her arms outstretched. She has a look of pure joy splashed across her face.

I can't help but feel the love.

Chapter Nine

A bunch of years later.

Jack's Flashback

I stopped drinking for a few weeks at a time. That's when I would convince myself that there was no problem. I would joke to anyone who would listen, "I don't have a drinking problem. I got no problems drinking." I convinced myself that I had it all together because I was still making good grades. But just when I started to feel like I had it under control, something in me would snap and I would find myself out of control. It's like I had this monster living deep within me and I tried to keep him hidden, but every once in a while he just had to come out to party.

I hung out with some serious drinkers who got loud and raunchy. The problem was they knew when to stop. I didn't. I would morph into the life of the party. I'd feel really good at one point in the night, like I was on fire. But the next day, I would be desperately searching every corner of my dorm to find my wallet or my phone. People who were my friends the night before, were no longer talking to me. I would have no idea why. When I tried to recall the night, I couldn't remember any details. Girls would look at me like I had broken their hearts, but I had no recollection of anything. After a night like this, it would take me weeks to get back to where I had been. I lost friends, money, phones, keys, clothes, time, and who knows what else?

After each drinking episode, I would think how much better off Lacey truly was without me. I began to give up on the idea that I could ever really quit drinking. And that made me start to really hate myself. It made me feel weak and out of control.

I kept tabs on her through Breck. He let me know when she graduated high school, what colleges she got accepted to, and when she moved to the big city to start attending Columbia University for journalism. I couldn't believe she was going to college in the same city as me. I wanted to see her, but I knew that if I couldn't stay sober, I had no right to see her. That was that.

I wanted to reach out to her when Gramps died. I just couldn't get her involved in my crazy antics. I wanted to reach out again when James and her mom had another baby. I wanted to be a part of her life, but I knew that it was an all or nothing deal.

Toward the end of her freshman year, I had heard that she had a steady boyfriend. Some dude named Rory, who was a bit of a musician and a bit of a mad scientist. Breck said it wasn't too serious, but I didn't know what to believe. He said he'd met the guy a few times at the house, but he didn't think Lacey was that into him.

"I remember how she looked at you. Believe me, that's not how she's looking at this guy. You don't have anything to worry about," Breck had told me.

I just hoped that he was a good guy. Lacey deserved that.

One day in my third year at NYU, something huge clicked in my brain. I realized that I was running out of time. If I wanted to have a good life, I had to get clean and sober. That was all there was to it. I had to stop fooling myself. I tried to cut out the partying in my life for good, but I could not do it alone.

I started seeing a therapist, going to AA meetings, and working out whenever I felt like hanging out and partying. My life became very scheduled, disciplined, and organized. It was the way it had to be. Every hour of my day was accounted for. It had to have a purpose. After a while, things became clear to me. I had definite goals and I knew that if I wanted to achieve them, I would have to stay sober for good. This would be my life from now on. I wasn't ever going back to drinking. I promised myself.

It was a difficult time. I slipped up a few times and had to start from the beginning again. I changed a lot. I became quiet and withdrawn. For a time, I stopped communicating with my parents. I felt like I just needed a break from their bullshit.

I always wanted to run a restaurant. My roommate had a friend who had a cousin who owned a café in the Village. The guy was moving to Florida and needed to sell the place in a rush. It was in a great location and the place needed very little work. I had saved a lot of money from all the construction jobs that I had done with Uncle Aiden. As soon as I saw the place, I knew it was a smart investment. I fixed it up myself. Five months later, restaurant critics were saying, "The Cozy Nook is the go-o joint for juicy burgers and meaty sandwiches."

Owning the restaurant was a dream that became a reality. This made me realize that it was possible to succeed. That's when I started finding my way back to my parents. There's still plenty of room for improvement, but at least now I can sit in a room with my mother without wanting to hurl things at her.

That's right about the time that Breck told me that Lacey was single again. Rory had been history for a while, and Lacey had been dating other guys, but she wasn't serious about anyone.

"You gotta call her," Breck said to me on the phone.

"I don't know, Breck. So much has happened. I don't know if it's fair to her," I said. "What if I can't stay sober? I don't want to hurt her ever again."

"Do you love her?" asked Breck.

I didn't hesitate. "Of course I love her," I said.

"You've turned your life around, Jack. Now get the girl," Breck said

I wanted to. Believe me, I wanted to.

"You owe it to yourself, Jack. That's all I'm going to say. You owe it to yourself," he repeated many times.

So one Saturday afternoon, out of the clear blue, I just found the courage to call her up. She answered on the second ring.

"Hey," I said. "It's Jack."

There was a long pause.

"Hi Jack," she said. And then I could almost hear her smile. "What are you doing?" she asked.

"Just hanging out."

"Oh yeah?" she said.

"Yep," I said.

"Well it's good to hear your voice," she said.

"You sound great," I said.

"So, I guess you heard that I go to school in the city," she said.

"You're a Columbia girl," I said.

"That's right," she said.

"Good old Breck," I said.

"So I heard you bought a restaurant. Cozy something, right?" she said.

"Good old Breck," I said.

"Yep," she said.

"It's called The Cozy Nook," I said.

"I'd love to try it out," she said. "I'd love to take you there," I said.

"It's a date!" she said.

"Hey, would you like to grab a cup of coffee?" I asked.

And then I waited to hear her say something like, "it's just not a good idea," or "I'm a little busy with my new boyfriend," or, "I'd like to go, but I don't have the time."

"Sounds perfect," she said. "How about Starbucks?" she asked, again I heard that adorable giggle of hers.

"Great idea!" I said.

An hour later, she was standing in front of a Starbucks in the Village.

She looked amazing. Her shoulder length hair was now a big frenzy of brown curls. Her face was pretty enough to be splashed in a fashion magazine. She wore lots of bracelets and a thick silver chain around her neck. Her black cowboy boots reminded me of the ones she used to wear. Her short jean skirt and tight black top looked really good on her. Everything about her was amazing.

When she saw me, she walked toward me and held out her hands. She smiled first, and then I smiled. It was like we were sharing one huge grin.

I moved in for a kiss and the sparks came.

OK. Now it's time to be in the moment. No more looking back. Time to look forward. She is dressed in white lace. My bride approaches. Her diamond wishbone necklace sparkles against her skin. The sparks are flying.

THE END.